Gorillaz in the Trenches 3

SAYNOMORE

Lock Down Publications and Ca$h
Presents

Gorillaz in the Trenches 3
A Novel by *SAYNOMORE*

SAYNOMORE

Lock Down Publications
Po Box 944
Stockbridge, Ga 30281

Visit our website @
www.lockdownpublications.com

Lock Down Publications
Like our page on Facebook: Lock Down Publications @
www.facebook.com/lockdownpublications.ldp
Book interior design by: **Shawn Walker**
Edited by: **Kiera Northington**

Stay Connected with Us!

Text **LOCKDOWN** to 22828 to stay up-to-date with new releases, sneak peaks, contests and more…
Thank you.

Submission Guideline.

Submit the first three chapters of your completed manuscript to ldpsubmissions@gmail.com, subject line: Your book's title. The manuscript must be in a .doc file and sent as an attachment. Document should be in Times New Roman, double spaced and in size 12 font. Also, provide your synopsis and full contact information. If sending multiple submissions, they must each be in a separate email.

Have a story but no way to send it electronically? You can still submit to LDP/Ca$h Presents. Send in the first three chapters, written or typed, of your completed manuscript to:

LDP: Submissions Dept
Po Box 944
Stockbridge, Ga 30281

DO NOT send original manuscript. Must be a duplicate.

Provide your synopsis and a cover letter containing your full contact information.

Thanks for considering LDP and Ca$h Presents.

Gorillaz in the Trenches 3

Chapter 1

"Buck Shot, loyalty is a two-way street, you can't be loyal to two masters, a lot of niggas in the streets don't understand that. All they see is the money, but loyalty don't have no face like money. When niggas learn that... there's no limit on how far they can go." Buck Shot passed the blunt back to Pillz as they talked in the park.

"So, you telling me you need some more loyal troops out there in the streets?" Pillz pulled his gun out and placed it on his lap. Buck Shot looked at him.

"No, I don't need no more troops out there on the streets, I need to clean house first."

"What you mean?"

"Rule number three, disloyalty will get you killed." Buck Shot looked at Pillz when he said that, but before he saw it coming, Pillz jumped off the table and shot him three times in the chest. Buck Shot fell on the ground on his side. Pillz looked at him.

"Money paid you to kill A-dog, and what you did in the dark came to the light. Like I said when we first started talking, you can't be loyal to two masters." Pillz pointed the gun at Buck Shot's head and pulled the trigger, killing him. Pillz walked out with his hoodie on, smoking his blunt and leaving Buck Shot in a pool of blood, dead with his eyes open.

***

"Pillz, did you hear the news?" Monay asked him as he walked in the house. Pillz walked up to her and gave her a kiss on the forehead.

"No, what news?"

"Buck Shot's been killed, it's all over the news. It's on now." Monay walked Pillz into the living room, where the TV was turned on the news so he could catch the story on Buck Shot.

"Damn, when this happened?'

"Yesterday afternoon around two o'clock they said."

"Let me go make some calls to see what the fuck happened out there in the dance." Monay looked at Pillz when he walked off. She could tell something wasn't right.

***

Fat-tee stepped out the black Benz on Smith Street, where Dapp, Sha-p, Red Rum and Tory stood in front of a house, smoking a blunt.

"Browns, what the fuck is poppin, my guys?"

"Shit, out here getting to this early money," Dapp said to Fat-tee.

"I ain't mad at you, baby boy. Get da bread."

"So, what brings you on the block? Hopping out the clean black on black Benz."

"I'm just out here showing love to my niggas, that's all."

"Already, homie."

"Yo Dapp, come take a ride with me."

"Come on, we out, family." Dapp got into the Benz with Tee and passed him the blunt, as Fat-tee pulled off.

"What's rocking, Tee?"

"I'm thinking you might need to take these streets over. Don Killer did it, Murder did it, A-dog did it, but they all fucked up when they started to beef with each other. You can't get money and have shells flying at you at the same time."

"I'm on the block pushing five- and ten-dollar rock bags. I don't even have a plug to supply the hood with weight, so how could I take over something if I can't feed the hood?"

"Pillz is the plug, so there is the answer to that problem."

"Pillz is fucking with Munchie on the work right now super hard."

"Yeah yeah, I heard that, but Pillz is about money. Check this out, Pillz owe me a big pussy fat favor, so let me take care of Pillz and you get ready to take over the blocks." Dapp looked out the window of Fat-tee's Benz as it started to rain.

"If you doing this for me, what's in it for you?" Fat-tee looked at Dapp.

"Twenty percent of the blocks. I wash your hands you wash mines, let's call it a mutual respect thing between the two of us."

"I can respect that."

"Let's get this money then, baby."

"Already." He pulled back up on Smith Street.

"I'ma pull up on you in a few days, homie."

"I'll be waiting, fam." Tee gave Dapp a pound before he got out of his car.

***

Munchie sat in Pillz' car and handed him a black duffle bag. Pillz opened up the bag and was looking at stacks of money on top of each other.

"What is the count, on the head?"

"Ninety thousand on the head for the two and a half kilos."

"Copy that, so you need two more?"

"Yeah, I do, fam."

"Cool, be looking out for me around eight tonight."

"Say less, I'm out, fam." Munchie got out the car. Pillz looked to see his phone going off, and it was Fat-tee calling him.

"Yo Fat-tee, what's the business, fam?"

"I'm calling in for that big pussy fat favor you owe me."

"Word, word… so you want me to pull up on you?"

"Yeah, come through tomorrow around two pm."

"I'll be there."

"O-killer." Pillz hung up the phone and headed back to his spot.

Chapter 2

Monay was on the bed watching *Lifetime* when Pillz walked into the room. He walked up to Monay and Gave her a kiss on the forehead and placed his hand on her stomach as he sat down next to her on the bed.

"Black queen, it looks like your stomach is ready to pop."

"I can't wait. I don't believe I let you destroy my body like this."

"Look at it this way, there's nothing more beautiful than a woman with child."

"It's easy for you to say, you don't have to look in the mirror every day at what used to be an hourglass figure."

"It's only a few more weeks before our little baby girl pops out of there."

"Lord knows I can't wait. So, did you find out what happened to Buck Shot?"

"No, the streets ain't talking but I still have a team looking into it right now."

"Good, because Buck Shot was loyal."

"Don't worry, I'ma handle the business, bae. I just came home to check on you. I have to go see Fat-tee. I'll be back in a few hours, bae."

"Oh, I'll be here when you get back, still watching my TV shows." Pillz kissed Monay on the cheek before getting up walking away.

***

Pillz walked up to Fat-tee and gave him a pound as he walked into his front door.

"What's rocking, my guy?"

"Shit… getting high, making money, Pillz."

"So, what's the big pussy fat favor I owe you?"

"I need two kilos from you, for the low."

"This is what I can do for you. I'll give you one, for what you did for me. And I'll sell you the other one for thirty-four G's, how that sound?"

"That sounds like a win-win for the both of us."

"Already, so when are you trying to do the business?"

"Today, hold up a minute, let me go get that cake for you. I'll be right back."

"Copy that." Pillz sat at the table, then he pulled his phone out and texted Ice-Berg to see if he needed some flour bags. He only wanted to make one run, he wanted to kill two birds with one stone.

"Check this out, playboy, thirty-four on the head. All big faces." Fat-tee handed Pillz the money as he walked to the counter and pulled the blunt out of the ash tray and relit it.

"I'll be back in a few hours, let me go take care of the business and make this other run real quick, homie."

"Just hit my line when you are on the way back."

"Say no more." Pillz walked out of Fat-tee's house to his car, headed to his spot.

***

"Dapp, come in and let me show you something that's sweeter than pussy, my nigga." Dapp walked into Tee's kitchen and was looking at the kilos of cocaine on the table.

"That's that butter right there?"

"Fucking right, ninety-eight percent pure. I'd like to call it the black takeover, a crack head's wet dream."

"What's the ticket on it?"

"Thirty-seven G's, plus my twenty percent but if you rock it out, you are going to make a hundred plus G's. Just off one."

"What's my window looking like?"

"Let's say ninety days with this package. So, it ain't nothing else to talk about then scrap, next time, see you. You should have a check for me." Tee passed Dapp the black book bag and looked at him. "Don't fuck up."

"I got this, homie."

"I know you do." Dapp walked out of Fat-tee's house with the book bag on his shoulders.

SAYNOMORE

Chapter 3

"Pillz, niggas been laying down for the last week and there's still no answers on who killed Buck Shot."

"That shit going to come to the light, but right now you need to keep a grip on the dance. If you are going to be in your emotions and can't hold the block down, let me know so I can put someone else in your place. Buck Shot had a graveyard on his Hummer, when you fire them shells, they fly right back at you." Pillz dapped Ice-Berg up before he stepped out of his car.

***

"What up, B-God? What's the word?"

"You know how the block talk. I'm coming to see if the pillow talking is true, Dapp." Dapp looked around and smiled and pulled a blunt out and lit it.

"I'm saying, what the block pillow talking about?"

"Word is you are the new kid on the block with the work."

"Yeah, that's a true story, what you looking for?"

"Let me get two of them twenty-eights off of you. What's the ticket on that?"

"I'm not even going to baptize you on the price. But that's going to run you twenty-two hundred and it's the color pink, so you can cut it two times, that's a crazy flip."

"Yeah, facts. Let's get that business out the way. I'm fucking with that price."

"Shit, follow me through the path, we are at the white house behind the school."

"Copy that."

***

Munchie watched as the black and purple Chrysler 300 pulled up on the block and stopped in front of him as the driver's side window rolled down. He smiled when he looked at Shorty Red.

"Hey, what's up, Munchie?"

"Shit, you tell me. You are the one pulling up on the strip bringing the sunshine with you, looking like the dime you are."

"I guess I am that bitch."

"Why the fuck did I just give you the big head?"

"Whatever, Munchie."

"Naw... but for real for real, how you doing today, baby girl?"

"I'm good, just riding around chilling. I see you are holding the block down."

"You know the money don't stop for nobody, so I got to get this paper while it's flowing.

"Shit, I be trapping. You going to put me on?"

"Baby girl, stop it. You already caked up. Shit, I'm trying to catch up to you."

"I'm trying to be like you and Dapp, them Brown boys is eating on both sides of town. Ya got the best of both worlds."

"What the fuck you talking about?" Munchie looked at Shorty Red funny.

"I thought you knew Dapp was holding the block down, and had all them niggas over there pushing weight for him."

"Hell to da no, I ain't know that shit, that's news to my ears."

"Well, I wasn't trying to start no shit, Munchie."

"Naw, you good, hands down, but check this out. Let me go make a run and I'll call you later on tonight, beautiful."

"That sounds like a plan, Munchie."

"That's the business then, be waiting on my call, beautiful."

"I will be." Shorty Red looked at Munchie and smiled before pulling off. Munchie pulled his phone out and made a call.

***

"What's dope boy talking about?" Ice-Berg looked at Realz and shook his head.

"He's on some backstage shit. He don't want niggas to make no moves. What the fuck is going on? He just want niggas to hold the block down till he gives us the green light to pop the bottle on whoever bodied son."

"Real shit, I heard the nigga who laid son down was from Amityville and it was about that A-dog shit."

"So, you think he might be holding back because he might know son?"

"I don't know all of this shit is funny to me. I don't trust the motherfucker right now, on gang."

Let me look into some shit and do my own investigation, and if this nigga is hiding something, we going to send his soul up in the clouds."

"Copy that." Realz dapped Ice-Berg up before walking away.

SAYNOMORE

Chapter 4

Jake walked into Manny's office, who was on the phone when he walked in. Jake took a seat in front of his desk to wait till Manny was off the phone.

"Let me call you back, nation. I have to take care of something." Manny hung up the phone and lit his cigar as he looked at Jake.

"So… I had Kent—who used to work for Omar—put some foot work in for us. Take a look at these pictures." Jake passed Manny a yellow folder with pictures of Pillz inside.

"So, who am I looking at?"

"They call him Pillz, he is supplying Amityville right now." Manny looked at the pictures of Pillz standing outside, talking with a few guys smoking weed.

"The guys he is talking with, are some of the guys he is supplying."

"The question is, where is he getting his supply from?"

"I'll show you where i think he is getting his supply from in a few seconds, but first look at these pictures." Jake handed Manny another folder, with five pictures of Tuggy dead, tied up on a pole. Then there were three pictures of an officer shot to death.

"Who is this I'm looking at. The dead cop?"

"Kent told me that two weeks before Tuggy was killed, he saw Monay in the bar talking with this officer, and not even three weeks after Tuggy was killed, this officer was gunned down."

"And this is the same officer Monay was talking to in the bar?"

"Yeah, the same one, Manny."

"So, what's the pictures in the third folder you are holding in your hands?"

"The answers to all of your questions." Jake passed the folder and Manny looked at the pictures of Pillz and Monay holding hands, side by side walking in the park.

"So, you asked me who is his supplier, I think the answer is right in front of your eyes."

"Omar was killed seven years ago, that supply would have been gone by now."

"Yeah, you are right, but think about this. What if she ain't pull it out for three to five years? And the product was ninety-eight percent pure, she coulda cut it three times and that would have been close to nine hundred kilos of coke. Cocaine sixty-five to seventy percent pure, so she would still have a great number of it today."

"I think it's time we have a talk with Monay."

"I'll reach out and see what I can do." Jake knocked on the desk one time before getting up and walking away.

***

Munchie walked up Smith Street to Dicey's house where Dapp was, watching the dice game smoking a blunt.

"Dapp, what's the word, fam?"

"Shit… getting money, playing the block, just normal every-day shit. How's your vibe going on today?"

"I really came to rap with you for a second, homie."

"What's on your mind, my guy?"

"Word is you got the weight, so I'm thinking you hold down Albany Avenue and Smith. I got the Flat Tops and we both eat without stepping on each other's toes."

"Man, it don't matter if you are over here, and I'm over there. This shit is going to sell, so we don't need no blocks or turf, that shit is crazy as fuck. It's enough money out here for the both of us."

"Check this out, Dapp. You just stay over here, and I got the Flat Tops, and we going to kill this shit off like that."

"Nigga, that's a demand? You got me all the way fucked up boy. You need to step, before I take this conversation another way."

"I think I'ma step off, I'll see you around, B."

"Yeah, do that, nigga." Dapp watched as Munchie walked off headed down Smith Street.

"Fuck nigga," Dapp said under his breath.

***

Two Weeks Later

Pillz looked through the window at his little girl as she laid sleep in her crib. Monay was sound asleep in their bedroom in the next room over. His daughter was beyond beautiful, she was innocent. She was his Promise, the reason for him to leave this life behind. He promised himself she wouldn't grow up without a father due to death or prison. He walked in the room and looked at Monay sleeping, he sat on the bed next to her.

"Baby, wake up." Pillz placed his hand on Monay's shoulder and rubbed her gently. She opened her eyes and looked at him.

"Are you about to leave?"

"Yeah, bae, I have some runs to make. I'll call you in a few."

"Ok, where is Promise at?"

"She in her room asleep, I just checked on her." Pillz leaned over and kissed Monay on the forehead before walking out the room.

***

"You see them niggas standing in front of the green house, Realz?"

"Yeah, I see them posted up like shit is sweet."

"While we are about to open they whole fucking chest up."

"Ice-Berg, niggas are going to feel us. On the set Buck Shot ain't going to die alone."

"Let's set this shit off." Ice-Berg and Realz put their Murder one masks over their faces and rolled down the window. As they looked at Dapp and his homies standing in front of his trap talking shit and smoking weed, Dapp looked at the black SUV flying their way.

"Oh shit, drive-by, drive-by." Dapp ran behind a parked car as Drums pulled his gun out and started shooting at the black SUV. Bullets were flying and all that was heard was the sound of gunshots. Drums got shot two times in the chest. Dapp jumped from behind the parked car and shot out two of the SUV's windows as it made a right on to Albany Avenue, hitting Sunrise Highway. Dapp walked up and looked down at Drum's dead body and shook his head. He picked up his gun and took off through the path off Smith Street before the police came to the block.

Chapter 5

"Sha-p, this shit is crazy, niggas pulled up out of nowhere blasting in a black SUV. They bodied the homie Drums, shit ain't adding up right now."

"Yo Dapp, you think it was Munchie?"

"Dead ass, it might have been that fuck nigga, he pulled up sideways two weeks ago. I let him know what the business is, then niggas come through spraying the block up. Now shit is adding up."

"So, what are you going to do now?"

"What the fuck you mean what I'ma do now? I'm gon lay this nigga down, on Browns." Dapp looked at Sha-p and put his hoodie on. and walked out the door of her spot.

***

"Ice-Berg, you saw how that fool hit the ground when them shells ripped through his ass?"

"My guy, that was a box office hit, how that movie played out."

"Copy that shit, two times, we ain't talking."

"Look, make sure them niggas are holding the block down, Pillz will be here on the strip in about two hours."

"Re-up time?"

"Facts, niggas is running low on that last bird. So, we need to break this nigga off with this paper, so we can get this cake and keep feeding the block."

"Let me go check on that shit right now."

"Say less, homie."

***

Pillz got pulled over on Sunrise Highway. He looked in his review window and saw one officer walking up to his Jeep. He rolled his car window down and pulled out his ID as the officer approached his car.

"Sir, do you know why I pulled you over?"

"I'm not a mind reader so I don't know." Pillz looked at the officer, as the officer looked around. The officer then pulled a card out of his jacket and dropped it inside Pillz' Jeep on his lap.

"You have seventy-two hours to call this number, or the next time I pull you over, you're going to take a ride with me. And we ain't going to no police station. So, if I was you, I'd call that fucking number. And next time, do a correct signal change and I won't pull you over. Have a good day, sir, take care." Pillz looked at the officer as he walked back to his car, then he looked at the number on the card he was given. The card did not have a name on it, just a number. He put the card in his glove box and drove off.

***

Dapp pulled up in the Flat Tops and stopped at the corner as he looked at Munchie sitting out front the house, talking with a few homies from the Flat Tops, drinking a forty-ounce of beer.

"Munchie, shit is crazy. I know you heard about how shit went down on Smith Street."

"I don't got no talk game for none of them niggas. I heard about what went down on Smith Street, and I gives no fucks about that fool who got bodied. I ain't going to stress or loose no sleep over that fuck nigga."

"Dead ass, I feel you, but word on the block is you sent them hittas at Dapp and them, and Drum's blood is on your hands. Long story short, you have a ticket on your head."

"Come on with that goofy ass shit, you dead ass?"

Don-don looked at Munchie and nodded. "You know I don't even play games when it comes to pistol play, that's why I really pulled up on you."

"So, Dapp think I sent niggas clapping at him?"

"I'm just saying the streets are talking, and your name is the main topic, you know how the hood headline news go. One nigga say it, and ten niggas run with it."

"What the fuck, and niggas is jacking that shit? On gang, I ain't send no shooters, but if niggas want smoke fuck it, flame on." Dapp cocked his gun back, rolled his car window down and hit the gas, doing sixty mph towards Munchie. Munchie looked up and saw the gun pointed out the window at him, he dropped his beer and took off running as Dapp fired shots at him and Don-don. Munchie jumped over the backyard gate. Dapp stopped the car and drove off around the block, trying to catch Munchie.

SAYNOMORE

Chapter 6

Pillz pulled his phone out and called the number on the card. He turned the radio down in his car as he waited for someone to pick up the phone, after a few rings someone picked up.

"Who is this? And why did you want me to call you?"

"Because your life depended on it. We need to talk face-to-face. Meet me at Amityville Beach tomorrow at three pm on the last dock. If you are not there, I'ma take it as a sign of disrespect and when we do meet, it's going to be more than a friendly conversation. So, if I was you, I'd be there." Before Pillz could say anything, the phone hung up. He put his phone in his pocket, opened up his car door and walked into his house.

***

"Dapp, I heard them rounds going off, what the fuck happened out there?"

"That nigga Munchie is straight pussy camel-toe, a straight bitch nigga, snake in the grass ass nigga. I do this shit for real. The fuck nigga hopped the gate in the Flat Tops, but I'm show his ass who the real animal is out here, that's on Browns."

"You know he's going to come back clapping."

Dapp looked at T-Millz and cut his eyes at him.

"And what the fuck is my heart supposed to do, pump Kool Aid? Let that nigga pull up. I'ma flat line his ass. I'ma show his ass this beef is real, till his ass is in a box like Drums."

"Copy that, but I'ma roll out, I'ma hit your jack later."

"Say less, homie." Dapp gave T-Millz a pound before he walked off.

***

"Dapp was just poppin at Munchie in the Flat Tops because he think Munchie had Drums bodied."

"Wait... you telling me them bulldogs going off was Dapp trying to roll Munchie?"

"Tee, dead ass, that shit just went boom."

Don-don sat at Fat-tee's table gun in his hand as he told him what went down.

"Fuck that boy. Dapp is a triple threat. Munchie ain't going to win this showdown."

"I don't know. Munchie was talking reckless like he ready for this shit."

"And that's why he's going to get his head crack. Let me try and hit this nigga Dapp up, because right now he's just killing time, but Dapp know the rules. kill him and keep it moving."

"So, what about me? That four pound was spitting shells at me too."

"Let me call this nigga. Stay low till I hit your line."

"Copy that."

Chapter 7

Munchie was looking out the window, holding his gun in his hand, smoking a blunt and waiting for Pillz to pull up. He put it on the hood he was going to body Dapp, and whoever the fuck he was with. Munchie saw Pillz' car pulling up, so he opened the front door for him to come inside.

Pillz walked into Munchie's spot and was looking at him as he held the gun in his hand.

"Man, what the fuck happened?"

"Your boy... your boy Dapp pulled up, emptying the clip because he think I had Drums rolled."

"Let me call the nigga to see what the fuck he got going on."

"Talk? How the fuck you sound? I just told you he emptied the clip on me."

"Nigga, you can't get money and beef, you trying to get money or beef?"

"Pillz, I ain't going out bad, Dapp just asked me to put him in a fucking bag." Pillz looked at the time on his watch, it was 2:20 pm.

"Look, Munchie, I have to go meet someone. Let me go take care of this business. Stay put till I get back, then we going to pull up and see what these niggas is talking about."

"Yeah, whatever, homie." Pillz shook his head and walked out of Munchie's house.

***

Pillz walked on the dock to see two men standing at the end of the dock, smoking a cigar and talking with each other.

"What's up? You called me, I'm here. What can I do for you?"

"I'ma get to the point, Pillz. I'm missing three hundred kilos of cocaine... do you know anything about that?"

"I don't know shit about that, and who the fuck are you?"

"My name is Manny, and this is Jake, and five years ago I got here I got robbed of three hundred bricks. Two years ago, someone killed two of my friends. So, I guess my one question is, who's supplying you for you to have enough product to take over Long Island the way you did?"

"Manny, with the utmost respect, I'm sorry for what happened to your friends, and I had nothing to do with your kilos being taken, but I'm not gone to reveal my supplier and I hope you can respect that."

"I do respect your loyalty to whoever you are dealing with, and I respect the fact that you came to see me alone. So I'ma leave you with these words. Every man who's been in Monay's life is dead, you should think about that." Pillz looked at Manny and Jake as they walked past him. Jake stopped and turned around and looked at Pillz.

"Money is a pretty face, but she is the devil and a demon and I'm sure she already had you walking through hell and trust me when I say this. No matter how many times you fucked her, you still don't know who she is." Jake pulled out some pictures and handed them to Pillz before walking off with Manny.

Chapter 8

"Ice-Berg, we ready for the re-up?"

"Fucking right, Realz."

Realz was smoking a blunt, while Ice-Berg was counting the money up at the table, getting the count together.

"We are going to pick up two of them birds, and I'm get him to front me one of them, I'ma stay on this side, you are going on the other side of the tracks, and we are going to lock this shit all the way down."

"Copy that. So Pillz is coming here?"

"No, I'm have him meet me at the trap over at the park."

"Why over there?"

"What's the point of having him come here, when we still have to bring the work back over there to break it down, cut it up and cook it up?"

"I guess, my nigga, any word from them Amityville cats?"

"Ain't shit come to me yet, but you know how that go. We did that shit smooth as hell, so nothing should come back on us."

"Who the fuck you telling?"

"Come on, I'm about to hit Pillz up now, to let him know what the business is."

***

Pillz was looking at the pictures of Monay, Omar and a few other people. She was plugged all the way in. It didn't take long to put two and two together. Manny wanted the streets and Pillz had the key to them. Pillz walked into the living room where Monay was watching TV, while Promise was asleep. He handed Monay the pictures and looked down at her.

"Is there something you ain't telling me?"

"Where did you get these from?"

"Manny and Jake, after they had one of they police friends pull me over to give me a number to call them."

"And when was this?"

"Two days ago, and I met with both Jake and Manny today."

"Why ain't you tell me this?"

"Monay, fuck why I ain't tell you this, why the fuck you ain't tell me you was mixed up with the cartel and that you was Omar's go-to girl?"

Monay stood up and looked at Pillz, upset.

"Do you know how the fuck it feels to be told what to do against your own free will?"

"Monay, we had this talk already, you just left out the key part, 'I work for the cartel.'"

"Because I hate who the hell I used to be, do you know who I was? Let me tell you. I was the bad bitch who would fuck you, suck your dick and cut your fucking throat from ear to ear. I had no feelings, fuck a nigga's life. That's what they made me into, I was whoever Omar needed me to be, Pillz."

"So, what about these three hundred kilos Manny is talking about?"

"Let me take care of Manny. I know how to deal with him."

"No, we will take care of Manny together, you're my wife and we will go into warfare together."

"And who is going to watch Promise?"

"Let me take care of that. But right now, I have to go take care of something in the Ville, so I'll be back in a little while."

"I'll be waiting."

Chapter 9

"Fat-tee, what's the word?"

"I'm trying to find out. I heard you was around here on your Billy the Kid shit, jumping out of cars and shit."

"Drums' blood is still on the streets, fuck that nigga life, on da gang."

"So why was you clapping at Don-don?"

"I don't have time to tell a nigga to get out the way. He did the right thing and let his feet kick his ass as them shells was flying."

"You don't need to make the block hot, wasting shells, missing your shot. Get the nigga down bad and take care of your fucking business."

"Man, that nigga going to bleed away when them rounds come out of that nickel plated and rip his chest open. I got the block, the bread still flowing. Shit good, Tee."

"I hope so, homie. I'm out, keep me posted."

"Already." Tee gave Dapp a pound before getting in his BMW and driving off.

***

Ice-Berg was outside when Pillz pulled up in Monay's white G-wagon, smoking a blunt with Realz.

"What's the word, my niggas?"

"Trying to ride like you, fam."

"Shit, we eating at the table together, ya time is coming soon." Realz passed Pillz the blunt as they went into the trap house.

"Yo, where your bathroom at? I have to take a leak. I been holding this shit since I jumped in the truck."

"It's the last door on the right, Pillz."

"Copy." Pillz walked into the bathroom, looked out the window and saw the black n SUV in the backyard, with the windows shot out. He used the bathroom and walked back into the kitchen where Ice-Berg and Realz were posted up waiting on him.

"My bad, I had to use the bathroom badder than a mother-fucker. So run this down to me, what you trying to do?"

"Buy two and get the third one on our face."

"Yeah, that shit is smooth. I can do that... you got the bread?" Pillz looked at Realz as he pulled the money out the kitchen drawer and placed it on the table.

"How much is that right there?"

"Seventy-four thousand bands on the head, fam." Pillz picked the money up and started counting it.

"Yo Ice-Berg, go check out them birds I have in the bag over there, while I finish counting up this cake."

"Cool, that's what the fuck I'm talking about, that pure co-caine." Pillz phone went off, he looked and saw it was Fat-tee telling him to pull up ASAP in the text message.

"Yo, I have to run but we good, just hit my jack when you have that check ready for me, Ice-Berg."

"That's without a doubt, homie." Pillz put the money in the bag and nodded at both of them as he walked out the door.

***

"You sure you want to do this, Munchie?"

"How the fuck you sound? This fool tried to off me... I want to knock this nigga block off. It ain't nothing to talk about. We here, Gunna."

"Sayless, homie. That's Shorty Red that just pulled up on the block talking to Dapp, yo. That bitch is playing both sides of the field. Shorty Red is foul as fuck." Munchie looked at her talking with Dapp, all in his face smiling as she sat in her car in front of his house.

"Yo, fuck that bitch, roll her too." Gunna pulled his gun out and smiled at Munchie as he put his Murder one over his face. Munchie hopped the gate and walked on the side of the house, with Gunna right behind him ducked down as they made it to the front yard.

"You ready, Gunna?"

"Yeah, let's do this shit."

Munchie ran from the side of the house with his gun pointed at Dapp. Shorty Red looked and saw Munchie. Before she could say a word, the sound of the guns going off echoed everywhere. Dapp turned around and got shot in his shoulder, hitting the ground. Munchie jumped the front yard gate. Dapp saw him coming, got up off the ground and took off running, with Munchie right behind him shooting. Gunna ran up to Shorty Red's car as she looked at him, letting off six rounds in her face as he stood next to her car, firing shots inside. Munchie stopped chasing Dapp and ran back to where Gunna was at.

"Damn homie, you took the bitch face off."

"I don't give a fuck... the bitch was two-faced anyway. Come on, let's get the fuck up out of here, before them boys come." Munchie and Gunna took off, back over the gate to his car parked on the next block.

***

Dapp ran to Sha-p's house, he was banging on her back door. Sha-p opened up the door and saw Dapp was shot.

"Dapp, who the fuck shot you?"

"Yo, I think it was that nigga Munchie. I couldn't see his face." Dapp was sitting down in a chair as Sha-p looked at his shoulder, trying to stop the bleeding.

"Dapp, you good, it went in and out."

"Can you stop the bleeding? I'm on papers, that hospital shit is a dub."

"Let me try some shit I saw... it might just work."

"Where the fuck you saw it at?"

"Just chill and let me do this, I'll be right back." Sha-p ran in the kitchen to the kitchen drawer, and then to the bathroom to the medicine cabinet. When she got back to the den, Dapp had his shirt pressed against his shoulder, to try and stop the bleeding.

"What the fuck you got there?"

"Dapp, are you going to let me do this? Or you want to do this?" Sha-p stopped and looked at him.

"Cool, do what you do."

"Thank you, now just relax and let me do this." Dapp closed his eyes and clenched his teeth as Sha-p poured alcohol on his shoulder, Dapp jumped.

"Damn, that shit burns."

"I know but I have to clean it, before I can do anything to it" Sha-p looked At Dapp.

"You might want to close your eyes for this part."

Dapp shook his head at Sha-p before closing his eyes. Sha-p opened the bottle of Super Glue and applied it on his wound as she squeezed it closed.

"Fuck! Fuck, that shit burns."

"Just chill, it's working, now let me do the other side." Sha-p got done and looked at Dapp. "You good, the bleeding stopped, it worked."

"What the fuck you put on it to make it stop?"

"Super Glue."

"Where the fuck you see that at?"

"A movie called *Black and Blue*."

"Yo, you just did some shit to me you saw on a movie?"

"Shit, it worked. It stopped the bleeding."

"Damn, them niggas had me down bad."

"Where was you at?"

"In front of my spot talking to Shorty Red. Fuck, let me go check on her."

"You sure that's a good idea?"

"I have to make sure she is alright." Dapp gave Sha-p a hug before going out the back door.

Chapter 10

Pillz pulled up in front of Fat-tee's house, who was outside parked in his driveway, talking on the phone. When he saw Pillz pull up, he got off the phone and stepped out of his car as Pillz walked up to him.

"What's rocking, fam?"

"Another day of the fuckery. Yo got wind of this bullshit Dapp and Munchie got going on?"

"Munchie was telling me something, but I had some other business I was dealing with at the time. What the fuck they got going on anyway?"

"I ain't hear this part from Dapp, but from what I was told, a black SUV sprayed the block up. Dapp shot it up, but Drums was killed in the shootout. Word is, Munchie sent the hit."

"That's why Dapp clapped at him and Don-don?" Fat-tee let out a deep breath.

"Yeah, that's why we need to go kill this beef before it get out of hand."

"Fuck it, let's go pull up on Dapp and see what he is talking about."

"We in your whip or mines?"

"We in mines, Tee."

"Cool, hit Smith Street, Dapp should be over there."

When they hit Albany Avenue, there were police everywhere, Smith Street was blocked off. All they saw was blue and red lights, and people walking around.

"Yo Tee, I think shit went boom already."

"Oh yeah, something must've popped off. Pull over by the church and let's see what the fuck went down."

"Damn, there's always some bullshit poppin off." Pillz pulled over and both of them got out the truck and walked over to the homies watching the block.

"What's all this shit about out here?"

"Tee, Shorty Red got bodied, and word is Dapp got popped." Fat-tee looked at Pillz and shook his head.

"Yo, who popped the bottle, SB?"

"Street news is saying it's Munchie, but that shit ain't stamped. Niggas wasn't out here; niggas is just saying that because they know the beef that's cooking between the two of them."

"I already know, SB, I already know. Pillz, come on and let's get the fuck up out of here."

"I'm already ahead of you on that idea, tee. Let's roll out." Fat-tee pulled his phone out and called Dapp but he didn't pick up.

"This nigga ain't picking up, I don't know what to say."

"Drop me back off at my spot. I have to get in my car and hit the block."

"Me too, fam."

Pillz dropped Tee off and called Munchie again. After a few rings he picked up.

"Where the fuck you at?"

"I'm in Bay Shore right now."

"Do you know what went down on Smith Street?"

"Come on, man, I was the star of the show."

"I'm on my way out there, I'ma hit your line when I'm close."

"Facts."

***

Monay had the babysitter watch Promise, as she went to see Manny. She pulled up at his detail shop, stepped out of her black BMW and walked up to the front door. Jake looked at her when she walked inside. "Where is Manny at?" Jake took his tongue and licked his teeth.

"In the back, follow me." Monay watched as Jake walked through the back door, she followed him to Manny's office. Manny put his cigar down when he saw Monay walk in. He walked around his desk to be face-to-face with her.

"How long has it been, Monay… fifteen years since we last seen each other?"

"And it still hasn't been long enough Manny. So, let's cut through the bullshit, what you want? And why do you have your pigs following my peoples?"

"We still want blood for Omar's and Pete. People get killed every day, and your people are no fucking exception."

"Likewise, Manny... stay out my lane and away from my peoples."

"You little mixed black and Cuban bitch. I have never liked you and if I find out you have Omar's blood on your hands, before I'm done with you, you're going to pray for death."

"Death don't frighten me, and your threats get my pussy wet. Remember, I put more bodies on the ocean floor, than the amount of times you hold your dick to take a piss. Pull up on my peoples again and we are going to see who door death be knocking on. Now test me, Omar." Monay turned around to walk out of Manny's office, when he called her name. She stopped and turned around and looked at him.

"This conversation ain't over with."

"It is." Monay turned back around and walked out of Manny's office, back to her car.

"Why you just ain't kill the bitch while she was standing here."

"Because I don't know who she came here with, or who she told she was coming here. Don't worry, Jake, that bitch day is coming... her lifeline is very short.

SAYNOMORE

Chapter 11

Pillz walked into the dimly lit house, there was soft music playing, and the inside of the house smelled like cinnamon. He looked up to the top of the stairs and saw Monay standing there with her hair down, with a matching bra and panty set on and three-inch red open toe heels. She had a dog chain on with diamonds in it. Pillz couldn't stop looking at her hourglass body, as Monay walked down the stairs to him in a sexy way, without saying a word.

She walked up and kissed him and started biting his bottom lip. She put her right hand in his pants and pulled out his thick manhood as she looked deep into his eyes. Pillz picked Monay up and carried her to the kitchen table, placed her on the table and opened her legs up. He started licking the inside of her thighs as Monay had her legs on his shoulders and her hand on his head.

"Baby, don't stop, just like that. Make this hot box cum, baby." Monay let out light moans as Pillz had his tongue deep inside of her. Monay started to move her hips up and down over Pillz' face as she was cumming. Pillz looked up at Monay with cum all over his face. Monay was taking deep breaths as she got down off the table, dropped to her knees in front of Pillz and placed his manhood into her mouth.

"Fuck Monay, wait… wait, baby."

"No! Stop running, I want to feel you in the back of my throat, baby." Pillz let out a loud moan as Monay was sucking on him, his eyes closed as he came in her mouth. Monay looked up at Pillz with the cum laying on her tongue. Pillz picked Monay up and carried her to the bedroom and laid her down on the bed as he placed himself inside of her. Monay wrapped her legs around Pillz' back as Pillz went deeper inside. Monay rolled Pillz over and got on top of him, riding him hard and moaning loud, cumming all over him again. They had sex for an hour before they got into the shower.

***

"Yo Dapp, I see the nigga came back blasting."

"Tee, that nigga dead, he just don't fucking know it yet."

"That's why you got all these niggas in the yard like you having a fucking yard sale."

"Shit got real the other night. Shorty Red got bodied, they took her face off, popped me in my shoulder. Shit don't stop till his face is on a tee-shirt."

"So, who got a hundred niggas with you to go catch a body?"

"Niggas know the drill, shoot or get shot."

"And you should know the drill too, half of these fools are going to be in court pointing they finger at you, when them number forty-plus come they way."

"My homies is loyal."

"John Gotti thought the same thing about Sammy the Bull, until he was sitting across from him pointing the finger at him."

"I got this, Tee, trust me."

"Trust you? Nigga, I don't trust the man i see in the mirror half the time."

"Say less, just know I got this."

"I hope you do." Tee looked at Dapp and walked back to his car.

Chapter 12

Munchie sat down smoking a blunt, talking to Gunna in the backyard.

"I'm still fucking mad at myself that I ain't kill that fuck nigga Dapp. I just couldn't get over the gate fast enough."

"Munchie, that nigga know what it is. I saw when you popped that nigga, I was hoping you killed his ass."

"His day is coming."

"I rode past his house yesterday and he had the house flooded with niggas. And guess who was in the yard with him face-to-face having a whole conversation, it looked like."

"The fuck if I know, who?"

"Fat-tee."

"You know what, I can go for that, and I'm willing to bet he's the one who put him on."

"So, you want to pull up on Tee?"

"No, fuck that nigga. I can't get mad because he got a nigga working the block for him."

"So what, we going to ride on Dapp again?'

Gunna passed Munchie the blunt and blew smoke out of his mouth.

"No, the block is on fire right now."

"Big facts. So where are we opening the next candy shop at?"

"Homie, we ain't moving our location, nigga pull up we blasting."

"How much weight we going to hold in the spot?"

"Just half a bird for now, we should be able to move that in four to five days top."

"Shit, you need to slide me that, so I can open the doors to the pot of gold."

"Pillz pulled up on me last night out here and told me he's going to slide me two of them today sometime."

"Copy that. Look, I'm about to push, homie. I'ma pull up on you in a few hours."

"Already." Gunna dapped Munchie up before walking off.

***

Pillz laid down in his bed and thought about what Fat-tee told him about the black SUV that shot up Smith Street. He didn't put two and two together at the time, but it hit him that the black SUV in the back of Ice-Berg's house was the same one that shot Smith Street up. Pillz sat up and licked his lips and nodded, thinking it was Ice-Berg who killed Drums for payback for him killing Buck Shot. He got out the bed and dressed. Ice-Berg crossed the line and Pillz was going to show him, and whoever he was with at the time, how it felt to take your last breath.

***

Ice-Berg was watching the basketball game at the park when Realz walked up.

"What's the move, homie?"

"Shit, what them niggas talking about on the other side of the track?"

"All them niggas see is dollar signs, they ready for me to open up the candy shop."

"Who you bringing over there with you? You know them niggas can be foul when they want to be."

"Shit, I'ma bring .45 and baby 9 with me, and if niggas start talking crazy like they jaw is broke, I'ma let .45 and baby 9 answer their questions."

"That sounds just about right. So, you want the whole bird?"

"Facts, I'm ready to flood that side of town, and Get that cake"

"Say less, fam. As soon as the game is over, we can go take care of the business." Realz looked at the little homies playing basketball.

"How much you have on the game, Ice-Berg?"

"Six hundred, and my team is up by twelve points and it's only eight minutes left in the game."

"Your little homies is in the black and white?"

"Yeah, big facts." Pillz pulled up at the park in the black Jeep and was looking at the many people watching the game. He never stepped out of his truck, he took pictures of Ice-Berg and Realz standing outside the gate watching the game, he had a trick for both of them. They didn't know but they were soon going to have a face-to-face with Buck Shot. Pillz wanted everything, the money from the three bricks and their lives, and he had just the bitch to trick them out of both. Pillz' phone went off and he saw it was a text from Monay, so he pulled out from the park and headed back to the house.

SAYNOMORE

Chapter 13

Pillz looked at Promise sleeping when Monay walked up behind him, placed her head on his back and wrapped her arms around him.

"Where was you? I was missing you."

"I went to see Ice-Berg and Realz, what you wanted to talk to me about?"

"Moving... we have more than enough money to move any-where we want, and to live comfortably. I just think it's time to leave New York and for us to start a new chapter somewhere else."

"What you have in mind, L.A., Georgia, Florida?"

"So, when you trying to move?"

"I don't care if we move tomorrow."

"You know niggas on the block in the Ville and Dance still owe me close to a hundred and fifty stacks still."

"Baby, we have millions, let them keep the pennies."

"You dead ass, bae?"

"Yes, I am. And it's not just for me, but for Promise. I don't want her to be a part of this life we live."

Pillz turned around and looked in Monay's eyes.

"So, how about you take Promise and go to L.A. tomorrow, stay for a few weeks just to feel it out to see if you like it or not."

"No... me, you and Promise can go as a family this week together." Monay looked up at Pillz and waited for him to say something.

"That's cool, get the plane tickets for us and make the reservations at a five-star hotel, and let's fly out to Cali."

Monay jumped in Pillz' arms and kissed him on the lips.

"I'ma go do all of that right now."

"Ok bae, I'ma be right here with Promise." Monay smiled and walked off.

***

Fat-tee was riding down Albany Avenue, when he saw Diamond walking down the street. He pulled over to give her a ride. She smiled when she saw his car and walked over to his window.

"Hey, what's up, Tee?"

"Shit, beautiful, you need a ride? Get in, baby girl, I got you?" Tee smiled as she got into the car.

"So, where you trying to go?"

"Over the bridge on Great Neck Road, right before we hit 110."

"Shit, what's over there?"

"My nigga lives over there."

"Who you fucking with?"

"Gunna crazy ass." Fat-tee looked at Diamond and reached into his ashtray, pulled his blunt out and lit it up.

"Tee, that's that gas, let me hit that."

"What would your man think about you smoking with me… plus giving you a ride home? No, my bad, his spot."

"That's my nigga, not my daddy, I do what I want to do."

"Show you right." Tee passed Diamond the blunt and just looked at her.

"You must think I'm a good girl. I do niggas the same way they do bitches."

"I hear you, Diamond. Where your nigga live at? We here over the bridge."

"Pull over next to that brown house on the right."

Tee pulled over and looked at Diamond and took the blunt from her. Diamond leaned over and pulled Tee's dick out and started to suck it. Tee closed his eyes and leaned back in his car as Diamond was deep throating him, putting all ten inches down her throat.

"Damn baby, what the fuck? I'm about to bust, damn girl, don't stop." Diamond kept on sucking on him until he filled her mouth up with cum. Tee watched as she   swallowed every drop of cum and licked all around the head of his manhood.

"Damn Diamond, what the fuck? What's your number? We have to have another round, hands down."

"Give me your phone." Diamond looked at Tee and licked her lips.

"You still think I'm a good girl?"

"I think I want you with me every day of the week."

"We can talk about it. I'll call you later."

"Where your nigga stay at?"

"Next door to where we are parked at now." Diamond Got out the car and walked off. Tee pulled off, headed back to his spot.

SAYNOMORE

Chapter 14

"Baby, it is so beautiful out here, I'm in love with L.A. already, I don't want to go back to New York." Monay was looking out the window as Pillz drove the rental car down the road.

"It is nice down here... so you talked to the agent about the house?"

"Yes, I told them we are looking for a five-bedroom house, with a full basement and a good school district for our little angel."

"Good, so what time are we meeting up with the agent today?"

"She said today at 3:00 pm and I have the address to the first house in my phone."

"Well, it's only noon right now, so let's go get something to eat and ride around somewhere to do more sightseeing."

"Ok bae, come on." Pillz looked at Monay and grabbed her hand as they drove down Avon and Carson City.

***

Munchie sat at the kitchen table cutting up the kilo of cocaine Pillz left him before he went to L.A. He knew he had to play the back scene with the beef him and Dapp had going on. With Pillz out of the picture, for the next two weeks he had to move smart, because anything could happen at any time. Munchie heard a knock at the door, he pulled his gun out and walked to the door.

"Who is it?"

"It's Gunna, homie." Munchie opened the door to let Gunna inside.

"Munchie, shit is crazy wild right now. I know I ain't tripping, homie."

"What the fuck is going on now, bro?" Gunna sat at the kitchen table and looked at Munchie.

"Dead ass, this bitch Diamond came to my spot high as fuck. So, we talking and kicking shit, she texted someone on the phone, then she start laughing. I asked her who she texting, she say her friend Monike. I don't pay it no mind, so we did us, I fucked her. She go wash up, I get her phone, she texted a nigga, talking crazy to him."

"What the fuck you mean talking crazy to him?"

"She told this fool, your dick is so big I couldn't even fit it all in my mouth, and you come a lot, I couldn't swallow it all."

"Damn, she foul as fuck, you got the number, right?"

"Fuck no, I got out of her message and placed her phone down, and the shit locked on me before I picked it back up."

"What you tell her?"

"I ain't tell the bitch shit, I want to catch her with this nigga and off them both."

"My nigga, you tripping, you talking about killing a bitch for sucking a nigga dick? Man, fuck that bitch and whoever dick she was sucking."

"It's about her trying me like a fucking duck."

"Homie, we getting this money and there's more badder hoes than Diamond. Throw that bitch to the side and pick up a new flawless piece."

"You right, you right… I'm tripping, fam."

"Facts, now help me count these grams up, Gunna."

***

"Yo Dapp, fuck doing a drive-by, we need to walk up and light his shit up. it's been two weeks since that fool popped you." Remo looked at Dapp as he sat on the hood of the car smoking a Newport.

"That nigga time is coming, the block is talking right now and real shit, that's how niggas get picked up on murder cases. I'ma let you know when it's time to pop on, son. But right now, let's just get to this baby love."

"Copy that, homie."

***

"Diamond, who pussy is this? You love this dick?"

"It's your pussy, Tee... your dick is stretching out my walls." Tee was biting down on his bottom lip as he was deep in Diamond, he started fucking her harder as she let out loud moans.

"Tee, daddy... oh my God, you have a big ass cock. I feel you in my stomach, daddy."

"You love daddy dick?"

"Yes... yes, I love daddy's dick." Diamond was biting down on Tee's pillow as he was hitting it from the back. When her phone went off, she reached to get it to see who was calling her. When she looked at her phone, it was Gunna calling her.

"Tee, wait! Wait... it's Gunna calling me."

"Pick the phone up then, you said you was a bad girl, right?" Diamond let out one moan right before she answered the phone.

"Hello?"

"Yo Diamond, we need to talk, where you at?"

"Right now? It's not a good time, Gunna. Let me call you back, baby."

"What the fuck you mean it's not a good time?'

"Gunna, it's not a good time. Daddy, you deep in my stomach, hmmm... I'm cumming... I can't take this dick! Fuck Tee, please pull out some." Diamond laid the phone down next to her as she let out loud moans. Gunna couldn't believe what he was hearing, Diamond was getting fucked while he was on the phone. All he heard was her moans getting louder and louder as he hung up the phone. In a state of rage, he grabbed his gun and put on the set he was going kill that bitch as he walked out the door.

SAYNOMORE

Chapter 15

"This is a big house and you said it's six bedrooms, a full basement, four bathrooms/"

"Yes, Mr. Kent, with a nine-foot swimming pool, the yard is gated off and the house is in a great school district."

"Ms. Moore, when can me and my wife come and look at the house?"

"How does tomorrow afternoon sound to you? Let's say 2:00 pm."

"That sounds great to me, we will see you then."

"Ok, I look forward to seeing both of you then."

"Likewise." Pillz hung up the phone and looked at Monay.

"Ms. Moore will show us the house tomorrow at 2:00 pm, bae."

"I really can't believe this is really happening, bae. We are moving to L.A."

"Believe it, bae… it's happening, we here."

Monay smiled as she looked at Pillz.

"Baby, are you happy that we are moving out here?"

"Monay, whatever makes you happy, makes me happy. That's all that matters to me."

"Baby, we did this together, through the blood, sweat and tears. It's time we enjoy the fruits of our labor. No more gunfights, murders or drugs, we don't have to look over our shoulders, just the three of us living peacefully."

"Listen, baby… I'm down for this, but I have to finish this unfinished business in New York, so you can pack up the house. And while you are doing that, I'll take care of what I need to do so when we leave, there's no looking back." Monay just shook her head and looked at Pillz.

"Ok, whatever, do what you need to do."

"Monay, don't say it like that."

"How do you want me to say it, Pillz? Fuck that unfinished business, fuck Amityville. We have a child now, that's the big picture I want you to see, we ain't living for ourselves no more, we are living for Promise." Pillz didn't say anything, he just looked at Monay as they headed to the beach house.

***

Gunna looked at his watch, it was 8:00 pm as he sat in the front of Diamond's house, waiting for her to come home. He got off her steps when he saw the blue headlights from Tee's BMW coming down the street.

"Oh, my fucking God! I can't believe this nigga is at my house!"

"You good? You need me to stick around, Diamond?"

"Let me see what he is talking about." Diamond got out the car and walked into her yard as Gunna walked up to her.

"That's the nigga you fucking, bitch?"

"Who the fuck you calling a bitch? Nigga, you better watch your fucking mouth."

"I'm calling you a bitch, you bum ass hoe." Gunna got up in Diamond's face and was pointing his finger at her.

"I know you ain't call me no bum ass hoe! you know what… I'll be that hoe, and that's why I had his dick all in my stomach, something I ain't feel with you since we been fucking." Gunna looked at Diamond as she sucked her teeth at him and tilted her head. Gunna looked at the BMW still parked there, looked back at Diamond and punched her in the face, knocking her down to the ground. Tee opened the car door and got out with a MAC-11 in his hand.

"You hit her again, you going to fuck up and die, nigga. You know who the fuck I am, nigga? Put your hands on her again, we going to see who bleeds first."

"You know what, fuck you and this bum bitch. I'ma see you again, nigga."

"I hope you do, motherfucker." Tee helped Diamond off the ground as Gunna walked out the yard.

Diamond got up and yelled, "You pussy nigga, I hope somebody kill your pussy ass. I fucking hate you. I hate you, nigga."

"Diamond, come on, let's get the fuck up out of here." Tee looked at her and helped her in his car. Diamond held her face as he drove off.

"Where you taking me?"

"My house, you can stay with me for a while, baby girl."

Diamond didn't say anything else, as Tee drove home.

SAYNOMORE

Chapter 16

"Yo Dapp, ain't that Munchie walking down Albany Avenue?" Dapp looked out the car window, at Munchie and someone else walking down the block.

"Yeah, that's that nigga, you know what time it is." Remo licked his lips and pulled his gun out and put his hoodie on.

"Let's do this shit then." When Remo said that Dapp punched the gas, headed towards Munchie. Remo put his flag over his face and pulled himself out of the car window to sit on the edge of the window. Dapp had his gun in his hand. Remo yelled while hanging out of the car, "You pussy."

Munchie turned around to see the sparks coming from Remo's gun. He pulled his gun out, ran behind a parked car, and started shooting back at the car. Dapp stopped the car and jumped out. Remo jumped out of the car window and was ducking down behind the car as he and Munchie was having a shootout in front of the school on Albany Avenue. Dapp chased Hut behind a white house, Hut didn't know Dapp was right behind him. Hut stopped running and turned around, while he was behind the house.

"I'm still here, nigga." Hut's eyes got big, as if he saw a ghost. When he saw Dapp pointing the 9mm at his face, all that was heard was Dapp's gun going off from a distance. Munchie and Remo heard the police coming. Remo jumped in the car and took off down Albany Avenue, where Dapp ran from behind the house and jumped in the car. Munchie looked up and saw the flashing lights coming his way and took off running between two houses with his gun in his hand.

"Yo Dapp, you good, fam?"

"Fucking right, I just rolled that fucking nigga."

"Munchie slipped through the cracks again, but he's going to get the fucking point."

"I already know you was taking care of the business, homie."

"Facts, you know how I do." Dapp looked out the window and saw they were good, the police weren't behind them.

***

Munchie pulled out his phone and called Hut two times, but he didn't pick up. He looked around and hopped two gates before he made it back to his spot. He locked the doors and laid back on the bed and closed his eyes as he tried to catch his breath. When his phone went off, he didn't even look to see who was calling, he just picked it up.

"Yoo yo, who is this?"

"It's Gunna, homie, you at the spot?"

"Fucking right, shit is bananas out there right now."

"Dog, who are you telling, the boys is everywhere right now. The streets is packed right now with blue and white."

"I know... that fool Dapp just tried to make a movie out of me."

"Word? I was Just about to tell you the street news, so you know they got the homie, Hut under the white sheet."

"Don't tell me that, I was just with son when shit popped off."

"It's over with, homie. That nigga hurt, he ain't coming back."

"You coming to the spot?"

"I'm on my way now."

"Hit me when you are out front."

"Copy that."

Chapter 17

Pillz pulled up to the white, two-story gated house, he and Monay stepped out of the car and walked up to the house.

"Hello, you must be Mr. and Ms. Kent?" Ms. Moore asked them. Before Pillz could say a word, Monay walked up to Ms. Moore and shook her hand.

"Yes, we are, and you must be Ms. Moore?"

"I am."

"Nice to meet you, Ms. Moore, this house is incredible, better than I could ever imagine. I love it already... bae, what do you think?"

"it's big, very big. I can't wait to see the inside."

"So please, come take a look. I don't want to keep the both of you waiting any longer." Ms. Moore walked Monay and Pillz into the house.

"Now, this is your living room, you have two fireplaces, your celling is thirteen feet high, you have wall to wall carpet, and there is two ways you can get into your kitchen from the living room. Come, let me show you."

Monay smiled as she looked at Pillz, he held their daughter Promise as he followed Ms. Moore into the kitchen.

"Now your counter and the island are made out of marble, isn't it beautiful, with the hard wood floor, and the window over the sink has an outstanding view of the neighborhood. Come take a look."

"Ms. Moore, you don't have to show me nothing else I want... baby, I want it."

Ms. Moore was just smiling, in shock that Monay wanted the house before seeing the rest of it.

"Ms. Moore, what is the asking price?"

"One point five million, is the asking price."

Pillz looked at Monay, then Promise. "Ms. Moore, we'll take it." Monay walked up to Pillz smiling, then kissed him and looked into his eyes.

"I love you, baby."

"I love you more, beautiful."
"Should we sign some papers? Mr. Kent?"
"Yeah, I think we should."

Chapter 18

"Manny, you wanted to see me?"

"Yeah, Jake, I did. Have a seat." Jake sat down in front of Manny's desk and looked at him as he smoked his cigar.

"I just got off the phone with Big Country. I told him about this whole Monay and Pillz thing, and everything else that's been going on up here for the last seven years. Long story short, he only had three words to say."

"And what was that, Manny?" Manny blew the smoke out of his mouth from the cigar, then looked at Jake.

"Kill them both." Jake nodded when Manny said that.

"I'll get on that right away Boss."

"Jake, I don't care if you make it clean or do it loud, just get it done." Jake nodded and got up and left Manny's office.

***

"This nigga Dapp, jumped out of a different whip, on me blazing, like this was a box office hit, and he was the star of the movie."

"Dog, when I pulled up out there, shit was crazy. I saw them put the kid Hut, in a fucking body bag, then you had the D's talking to schoolteachers and all."

"This fool trying to be the star in a movie, but I'ma show him this is real life, and I kill niggas for real."

"You know we got to take care of that business, the homie Hut is in an icebox right now."

"Come on, you know I ain't about to let that shit ride."

"Yo Munchie, let me tell you the flip side of some other shit, you ain't going to believe."

"And what's that, Gunna?"

"I called Diamond right."

"Here we go with the twenty-seven chapters of the Diamond story."

"What the fuck ever, nigga, but check this shit out."

"Cool, let me hear what you have to say, Gunna."

Munchie rolled a blunt up, as Gunna was talking to him.

"So, I called Diamond up, she picked up the phone and the bitch ain't even talking right. Then she start moaning in my fucking ear, like I ain't even on the phone. Then she tell the nigga, 'your dick is breaking my walls down,' on gang. I hung up the phone, I couldn't believe what I was hearing."

"Nooo, she ain't do it like that."

Munchie was laughing as he smoked the blunt.

"That's not all. So, I go to her spot, and punch the thot out, and guess who became a Super Save A Ho?"

"Who? My nigga, I need to hear this one."

"Fat-tee! Munchie, this nigga jumped out the BMW holding the MAC-11 talking sideways to me, like I'm straight pussy."

"So, what you say to that nigga?"

"I told him I will see him around, and I stepped off."

"So, you going to roll this nigga?"

"Fucking right."

"Then there is nothing to talk about, him and Dapp got that death wish they been wanting." Gunna nodded at Munchie as Munchie passed him the blunt.

***

"Yo Dapp, how that fool looked before you clapped him?"

"Like he saw a fucking ghost coming out of a grave. When he turned around and saw me, and I said I'm still here, that fool couldn't do shit as them shells pushed his shit back."

"Fucking right, bang-bang, my nigga. Nigga know who the fuck we are, and how we pulling up."

"Yo, look Remo, I ain't talking no more, it's shoot or get shot."

"Already! You ain't got no bud to roll up, Dapp?"

"Yeah, let me grab it real quick, homie."

"Copy that."

Chapter 19

"Baby girl, I'm about to head to the store, you want something?" Diamond pulled the covers down from over her head, to look at Tee, who was sitting on the edge of the bed, putting his boots on.

"Yeah, can you bring me back a breakfast sandwich, daddy?"

"Yeah, I got you, black queen." Tee leaned over and kissed Diamond on the lips before walking outside and looked around before getting into his car. Tee pulled out the driveway, when his phone went off. He looked and saw it was a text message from Dapp, telling him to pull up. Tee replied, *give me twenty minutes*, as he headed to his house.

***

Dapp was smoking a blunt when he got the text message from Tee. He walked into his room and got the money out the safe and counted it up before Tee pulled up. By the time he made it back to the living room, Tee was walking up to his door, he opened the door and looked at him.

"What's rocking, homie?"

"Shit, you got me over here early in the morning. I ain't even eat breakfast yet."

"Your big ass
look like you can miss a few meals."

"Dapp, what the fuck you want?"

"Big boss, just come inside." Dapp walked away from the door.

When Tee walked into the house, Dapp had his money on the kitchen table, he sat on one side of the table smoking a blunt.

"Yo, this is seventy-four racks, plus the twenty percent on your end. I told you I can spit shells at that fuck nigga Munchie, and still get to the bag."

"I already know you're a paper chaser, Scrap, but I'm trying to keep you out of them silver cuffs, and how you are moving, there's only two ways your story going to end."

"Yeah, I already know, with a hottie sitting on my face, or sucking my dick, either way it's a happy ending for me."

"Yo, you are too much for TV. Dapp, you still got more work left?"

"Yeah, I still got half a bird left."

"Cool, I'ma call Pillz and get two more for you. When I get them in my hands, they'll be in yours."

"Say less, big bro." Tee, gave Dapp a pound and hit his blunt before walking out the house.

***

"Ice-Berg, I heard the homie Pillz went MIA?"

"That's a true story, Realz. He told me he was taking a trip when he dropped them birds off on me, like two days after the B-ball game in the park."

"We straight on the work till he comes back?"

"Hands down, we are a hundred on that tip. But fuck all that, what's good with shorty saw you vibing with at the park with the pink on?"

"Man, come on, you know I broke that bitch back the same night. Plus had the wood in the back of her throat with the balls on her chin." Ice-Berg jumped off the hood of his car, where he was sitting and started laughing as he gave Realz a pound.

"Well, you know what they say, sharing is caring, because real shit, I'm trying to see what them cheeks is hitting like."

"Man, fuck that bitch, and that box is water. I had to pull out twice, just to make sure the condom was still on."

"Yeah, slide me that number, so I can give baby girl a ring."

Realz pulled out his phone and passed it to Ice-Berg so he could get the number out of it.

***

Pillz carried Promise into the house, laid her down in her crib and covered her up, while Monay brought their bags into the house from their trip. Pillz walked into the kitchen and poured himself and Monay a glass of peach soda and waited for her to come into the kitchen. As he sat down, she walked into the kitchen.

"Baby, I poured you a glass of soda, come have a seat and relax with me."

"Here I come right now, bae." Monay sat down at the table across from Pillz. "Baby, I can't believe we got the house, I can't wait to move into it."

"Beautiful, you know I would do anything for you and our daughter, no matter what I have to do to put a smile on your face."

"That's why I love you so much, bae. So now all we have to do is pack up the house."

"No, all you have to do is pack up the house. I did my job already. Now that I'm back home from L.A., I'm about to go do what Promise is doing and go to sleep." Pillz got up from the table, kissed Monay on the forehead and went upstairs and laid down to go to sleep. Monay looked around the house and closed her eyes. She couldn't wait to leave New York and leave her past behind her and start her new life in L.A. with the man she loved.

SAYNOMORE

Chapter 20

"What's good, Tee? I see Batman came out from behind the shadows."

"Sometimes it's good not to show your face and let the hood miss you."

"That's a true story."

"What the fuck you been up to, Mikey?"

"I'm just out here, listening to these niggas pillow talk on the block."

"And what these niggas talking about?" Mikey looked at Fat-tee and started laughing.

"What's so funny?"

"Word is that you have your hands in Gunna's cookie jar."

"Fucking right, and that bitch ass nigga could take it to the heart."

"Just watch your back, you know how niggas get over bitches."

"If that boy try me, you going to see that nigga face on somebody tee-shirt, with RIP on that bitch."

"I already know. If he do, he got a death wish to meet his maker."

"Son knows how I get down already. But let me get this food. I was supposed be back at my spot an hour ago."

"Say less, fam." Tee dapped Mikey up before walking into the deli. Mikey walked off down the street and saw Gunna, walking out of the Flat Tops.

"Yo, yo... Mikey, what's rocking, my guy? Tell me you got a light on you."

"Yeah, I got one, but you might want to walk the other way, homie."

"And why the fuck it that?" Mikey handed Gunna the lighter and watched as he lit his Black & Mild.

"Because Fat-tee is at EZ deli right now, and I know both of you have smoke with each other right now."

"Word? That fat nigga is on the strip right now? Yo, good looking, let me pull down there right now."

"Be safe, homie."

"Always." Gunna walked down the street and saw Fat-tee driving his way. He pulled out his gun and ran to the middle of the street and started shooting at his windshield. Tee turned into someone's yard and jumped out of his car, gun in hand. Gunna was still in the middle of the street, shooting at Tee as he was ducked down behind his car.

Tee yelled, "You dead, nigga! You done fucked up, you missed your shot."

"I ain't miss shit, nigga. I still got eighteen rounds in my F.N.M."

"If I don't die today, your mother is going to be looking down at your dead body tomorrow." Tee got up from behind the car and started shooting at Gunna, who ran behind a tree. Tee jumped in his car and took off down the street. Gunna ran from behind the tree and shot out Tee's back window as he was Driving off. Tee felt something warm running down his arm, that's when he realized he'd been shot, he started talking to himself out of anger.

"Fuck, I'm kill this nigga, Gunna." Tee pulled into his yard and got out his car gun in hand as he walked inside the house.

"Baby what took you so long?"

"Shit went sideways just now. Go to the car and get the black bag out the car, it's in the back seat." Diamond looked at Tee and ran to the car, as Tee went into the bathroom to look at his arm. Diamond ran back in the house with the duffle bag in her hand and went right to the bathroom where tee was at.

"Tee, what happened?"

"Gunna got me down bad, on gang, I'ma kill that nigga."

"You been shot, you have to go to the hospital."

"No, I'm good, it went in and out. Just get me some hot water and a towel." Tee had taken his shirt off and was looking at his arm where Gunna shot him. Diamond came back in the bathroom, with a hot towel and a pot of hot water.

"What the fuck happened out there?"

"Help me just clean this up and I'll tell you what went down."
Diamond looked at his wound and started washing the blood off
his arm.

SAYNOMORE

Chapter 21

Pillz walked to his nightstand and pulled out his 9mm, placed it in his waistband, and covered it up with his shirt. He looked at Monay still asleep in the bed, lying next to Promise. He walked outside to his car, there were a few things he had to get done. Pillz pulled out of his driveway, playing Lil Wayne's *John Doe* as he headed to see Munchie.

***

"Gunna, I know you ain't air the block out like you telling me you did." Munchie was looking at Gunna as he drank his forty-ounce beer.

"Dead ass I did, that fat fuck was coming down the block and I let that F.N.M. blow. I ain't doing no more talking. Fuck that nigga and Dapp, niggas know what beef is, and if they don't know, now they do." Munchie walked to the living room window and looked outside to see Pillz walking up to his door, smoking a blunt. He looked back at Gunna, and shook his head smiling, then he opened the front door for Pillz to walk inside.

"What's the word, Munchie?"

"Shit crazy out there right now. I know you heard about what the fuck happened."

"I just got back in town, what the fuck happened now?" Pillz looked at Gunna, as Gunna pulled his gun out and started to smile.

"The boy Gunna popped the bottle on Tee today, caught him slipping and popped his ass."

"Wait… hold on, you clapped Tee?"

"Fucking right, that nigga tried me over a bitch I was fucking, pulled the MAC-11 out on me and all, so off top you know I was on the fuck shit."

"Gunna, did you body him? That's all that matters right now, that's what I want to know."

"All I know is I clapped him, and he hopped in his car and put the pedal to the floor, fat boy was gone in sixty seconds."

"Gunna, you are a walking dead man, I don't think you know the line you just crossed."

"Pillz, I respect you, but that nigga bleed just like you and me."

"Yo, this shit is wild... look Gunna, I don't want to see you on the cover of a newspaper. Stay on point and keep that hammer on you at all times, you know what it is right?"

"It's beef."

"Yeah, so keep in mind it's shoot or get shot now, you draw first blood."

"Munchie, I'ma pull up later and bless you with some work."

"Cool, just hit my line." Pillz gave both of them a pound before walking out the house.

***

Dapp ran up Tee's walkway and was banging on his door. When Tee opened the door, he saw Dapp holding the gun in his hand, While Dapp looked at Tee's arm.

"You going to look at my arm, or are you going to come in the fucking house?" Tee moved out the way for Dapp to come in the house.

"What the fuck happened, fam?"

"Niggas wanted to show me I can bleed, and that my car wasn't bullet proof, I guess." Tee let out a light laugh.

"Tee, this shit ain't funny motherfucker tried to take your life.

"It's going to take more than an F.N.M. to stop my heart from pumping." Dapp shook his head in a sign of anger.

"Do you know who shot you?"

"Yeah, I do. Gunna, I want that fool body in a pool of blood." Dapp nodded.

"Let me go put a GPS on this fool, he shouldn't be hard to find."

"Just find out where he's at and I'ma take care of the business. This shit is personal, you get me?"

"Yeah, I do. But you know they kill you, they kill me… so this shit is personal to me too."

"I already know Scrap, hands down, I do."

"Let me go locate this fool."

"Yeah, do that for me, baby boy."

***

Pillz stopped at the red light on Sunrise Highway. He looked to the left and saw a black van pull up next to his car, there was an older white man inside the van. When Pillz looked down at his phone, that's when he heard the side door to the van open up with a loud bang. A man holding an AR-15 pointed it at him and before he could blink an eye, bullets were flying out of the gun coming through the side of his car door and breaking through his windows.

Pillz tried to lean over in the car as he pressed the gas, trying to take off, when another car ran head-on into him. The old white man jumped out of the van and started shooting Pillz' car up again. He stopped shooting, looked at Pillz' car with blood all over him. He was coughing up blood as he tried to hold himself up on the car. The old man pulled his gun out its holster, pointed it at Pillz, and shot him three times. Then he watched Pillz' body hit the ground before he got back in his van and pulled off.

***

Monay's phone went off, she rolled over to see who was calling her, it was an unknown number. She picked up the phone to see who was calling her.

"Hello?"

"Can I speak to a Miss Kent?" Monay pulled the phone from her ear when the male voice on the other end said that, to take a second look at the number that called her.

"May I ask who is calling?"

"This is Detective Moorehouse, with the 6th Precinct." Monay sat up when he said that.

"This is Miss Kent… how may I help you?"

"I'm calling because your husband, Anthony Kent, has been shot multiple times. He is in surgery as we speak being operated on. We need you to come to the hospital, Miss Kent, there is a strong chance your husband might not make it."

Monay couldn't believe what she was hearing,

"What… what you said, he's been shot?"

"Yes, can you come to South Shore Hospital in Bay Shore?"

"Yes, yes… I'm on my way there now."

"Ok, I'll be here when you get here." Monay hung up the phone, dressed Promise and rushed out the door to her truck. Her heart was beating a hundred mph as she rushed to the hospital.

***

Manny walked to the back door of the detail shop as Jake opened the garage doors. Manny looked on as the black van pulled inside. Jake peeked out the garage doors before closing them, the old white man stepped out of the van and walked up to Manny and shook his hand.

"How was the take-out, Jason?"

"To die for, the meal was well done."

"I knew you would like that menu."

"I can't wait to try the other menu, from the next five-star restaurant."

"As soon as I get the address, you will get the address."

"Call me when you ready."

"I will." Manny shook Jason's hand as he was about to leave the detail shop.

"Jake, did you witness the events today?"

"I did and let me say this, if he walks away from that, he had the whole armor of God on." Manny nodded as he looked at Jake intently before walking away.

***

Monay walked into the hospital holding Promise, she saw both detectives standing at the front desk, drinking a cup of coffee. She walked right up to them.

"Detective Moorehouse?" Detective Moorehouse looked at Monay, and couldn't believe how beautiful she was, he was lost for words.

"Miss Kent?"

"Yes, I am her, how is my husband?"

"I don't know, I'm waiting to hear from the doctor now. Do you know who would want your husband dead?"

"No, I do not know. Can we go see the doctor? My heart cannot take this."

"Sure, let's see if he's out of the operating room, come with me." When they reached the third floor, they walked to the waiting room. Monay had tears in her eyes as she waited for the doctor to come out of the operating room to let her know Pillz' condition. The thought of him lying on the operation table being worked on, with tubes going down his throat sent sharp pains to her heart. *Baby, I love you so much. Please don't leave me*, she silently prayed.

Detective Moorehouse walked up to Monay. "I'm sorry you are going through this. I know you love your husband, but there are some questions I need to ask you. And if you feel you are up to it, we have the video of the shooting from one of the video surveillance cameras, if you wish to see it." He intended to block out the images of Pillz actually being shot, but he wanted her to get a look at the vehicle the unknown suspect was driving, just in case she recognized who it belonged to.

Monay spoke in a low tone, "Yes, I want to see it." Monay watched as the doctor took his gloves off and walked to the sink and washed his hands, before walking out of the recovery room.

"Hello. Detectives… this must be Miss Kent?"

"Yes, I am. how is my husband coming along? And be straightforward with me please."

"Your husband is very, very lucky. He's been shot a total of six times, twice in the shoulders, once in the stomach, once in the leg and twice in his back. Three of the gunshot wounds were with an assault rifle. I believe the car door took a lot of pressure off the impact of the bullets that hit his legs from the assault rifle. The car door saved his legs, as well as his stomach. The other three shots came from a handgun. We got all the bullets out, but he lost a lot of blood, we had to give him two blood transfusions. It's gone to be a while before he's a hundred percent again."

"When can I see him?"

"Right now, he'll be taken to ICU. He is in stable condition, but it would be best to come see him tomorrow, Miss Kent." Monay let out a low breath.

"Ok, Doctor, you know what's best."

"Miss Kent, can you come down to the station so we can ask you a few questions and show you the video?"

"Sure, come on, I'm ready." Money kissed Promise on the forehead as she was asleep in her arms, as they walked out the hospital.

***

Miss Kent, as you can see, your husband pulled up at the light, and a black van pulled up next to him. A few seconds passed and you see the van door open, and it's at that point shots are fired from the inside of the van at your husband's car. Your husband tried to get away but ran head-on into this car. As you can see, the car your husband hit backed up and drove away after the driver saw the man get out with the gun in his hand."

Monay heard what Detective Moorehouse said, but she knew what had really taken place and she knew Manny pushed his little red button, but his shooter fucked the job up. Now they were going to see the real bitch Omar made, and she was going to send a message to Country to let him know she was still the same bitch he remembered.

"Detective, I've seen enough. I'm sleepy and I need to get Promise home and feed her, I really hope I helped with the questions you asked me, if it's all the same to you, I think I will go home now."

"You were a help, and here is my card, if you need me."

"Thank you, Detective Moorehouse."

"You're welcome, let me show you out." It was 11:30 pm when Monay made it home. She laid Promise down and pulled out her phone and made a few calls. She needed the babysitter to take Promise for the week, Then, she called her priest for him to say a prayer for her, because before all of this was over, Manny was going to be a dead motherfucker.

SAYNOMORE

Chapter 22

Monay walked into the hospital, right to Pillz' room in ICU. She looked at him sleeping, she leaned over and kissed his forehead, and placed a picture of him, her and Promise next to his bed on the end table.

"Baby, I know you can hear me, and I need you to fight through this for me and Promise. We both need you, baby. I have to go take care of a few things. I love you, Anthony Kent." Monay kissed Pillz one more time before walking out of the hospital room to her car.

***

Don-don was posted up in front of the Pinks, smoking a Black & Mild, making plays when Remo walked up on him with a black hoodie on, with his hand under his shirt holding his gun. Don-don took a step back and turned around, and Dapp walked up to him with his gun in his hand.

"Niggas really don't want no smoke with you, but I will take it thee with you if I have to." Don-don looked at Dapp with his gun in his hand, then back at Remo.

"Dapp, you know I don't have no smoke with you, I didn't even come at you sideways when I was out there with Munchie the day you was clapping at him, because I know that was ya beef."

"That's a fact too, but here's the problem with that. Munchie and that fuck boy Gunna is on the grocery list, and they are ducked the fuck off right now, and for some crazy reason, I think you know where he ducked off at. So I'ma need that information from, or I'ma have to add another name to that grocery list, you feel me?"

"Yo Dapp, you got to believe me when I tell you I don't fuck with that nigga like that. Tee been told me to fall back on that fool."

"I do believe you when you said you fall back from son, Tee told me you pulled up on him about that shit that went down, but just because you don't fuck with a nigga, don't mean you don't know where he lay his head at." Don-don shook his head from side to side and closed his eyes and licked his lips.

"Dapp, I ain't trying to send you on no blank mission to no fake address, I don't know where that nigga close his eyes at."

"Cool, it ain't no pressure. This is what I'm do, I'ma step off but next time I see you, have that address for me." Dapp nodded at Remo and both of them walked off, Don-don just looked at them and walked off the other way.

***

Munchie's phone went off, he looked and saw it was a message from Don-don, saying, *watch who you have around you, Dapp and Remo just pulled up on me the strong way at the Pinks, trying to find out where you lay your head at.*

Munchie replied back, *good looking on the heads' up Scrap, love my hitta.* Munchie got up from the table and walked to the living room where Gunna was At smoking a blunt watching, *Boyz N The Hood.*

"Yo Gunna, check this shit out, the homie Don-don. Just texted me this." Munchie showed Gunna his phone so he could read the text message.

"So, these niggas is going to the streets to try and find the lion's den? Munchie, these fools are pulling all cards."

"Yeah, I see that. We need to find them, before they fuck around and find us first."

"Real shit, I bet the homie Pillz can find out where the boy Dapp lay his head at."

"Gunna, I ain't hear from Pillz in two days, and I been blowing his line all the way up."

"You think he on some funny shit too?"

"Hell no, that's not Pillz' style, something else is going on with him. I just don't know what it is yet."

"So, intel then, what are we going to do about these nigga?"

"Shoot on sight, that shouldn't even be a question. But get ready. I need you to take a ride with me to the 40's."

"What's over there?"

"The last half a brick, I need to pick up."

***

Monay was parked across the street in a white two-door car, looking at Manny's detail shop. She'd been parked there for two days, each day she changed cars. She sat up closer to the windshield when she noticed a blue van come from the back of the detail shop, it looked just like the one that pulled up on the side of Pillz' car, it was just a different color. Monay started up the car and followed the van. She pulled her black 9mm out whoever was in the van, was going to deliver her message to Manny,

She pulled the black duffle bag from the back seat to the front seat and opened it up. For what she had in mind she knew she had to be fast, two to three minutes top, and she wanted it to be just like they did Pillz at the red light. Monay put the black face mask and hoodie on and pulled the machete out of the duffle bag. She looked around to see how many cars were around, it was only four. The van stopped at the red light on 110.

Monay pulled up behind the van, she looked around one more time, then opened the car and ran to the driver's side of the van door. When the driver turned his head, all he saw were the sparks coming from the gun, and the glass window shattering as the bullets went through, Monay opened the van door and pulled the driver's body out of the van, and shot him three more times, she took the machete and with three chops took his head off.

She ran back to the car with the head in her hand and pulled off, when she looked in the rearview windshield, she saw people out of their cars, realizing they were watching the scene as it unfolded. When she made it to the warehouse, she put his head in the duffle bag and set the car on fire, got into her black BMW and pulled off.

***

"Manny, you might want to come take a look at this." Manny looked at Jake and got up from behind his desk, and walked into the lobby of the detail shop, where the news was playing.

"You got to be fucking kidding me, how long ago this happened?"

"Not even two hours ago, someone had the whole thing on tape. She cut his head off, she wants us to know it was her."

"Look, Jake, they showing the video now." Manny watched the video of Monay. He knew who she was by the way she moved. But she was in all black, if you didn't know better, you would think she was a man. She was quick with the draw and fast, cutting his head off.

"You see the car she was in?"

"Yeah, what about it, Jake?"

"It's the same one that's been sitting across the street all day."

"She was watching us to see who comes and goes."

"Yeah, she was."

"The van was clean?"

"Yeah, from top to bottom."

"Go, find out where the bitch is at and kill her."

"I'll do that now." Manny nodded and walked back to his office.

Chapter 23

Tee got up when he heard a knock at the door, he looked and saw Dapp and Remo on his front steps. He opened the door for them to come in.

"Yo, shit is bananas, out there, y'all niggas come in and check this shit out. I'm watching on the news." Dapp looked at Tee with a funny face as he walked into the house.

"This shit just went down yesterday, whoever the fuck son is went ape shit, took the nigga head off in the middle of the street. I don't know what the fuck he did, but he fucked up big time."

"Fucking right he did, look me and Remo came over to let you know, these dude are really MIA. I don't know where the fuck they are at, and I'm low on work, I only have sixteen rams left."

"I called this fool Pillz a few times, his shit is going right to voicemail, I don't know what's going on with him." Remo looked to the right when he saw Diamond walk out the room in a pink set up. She was looking like Beyonce in the flesh. Diamond was a real showstopper. She walked up to Tee.

"Tee I'm hungry, can yo go get me something to eat?"

"Yeah, I got you, baby. Dapp, run me to the store real quick."

"Yeah, I got you, come on." Tee looked At Remo. "Yo Remo, post up with shorty till we get back, just in case a nigga tries to run up in my spot."

"Cool, no problem, homie." When Tee and Dapp walked out the door, Diamond looked at Remo and cut her eyes and licked her lips at him.

"So, you have to put your life on the line for me, Remo?"

"I'ma do what I need to do, if a motherfucker run up in here, I'ma send him to his maker." Diamond let out a smile.

"I'm glad to know I am safe with you." Diamond walked up close to Remo till she was face-to-face with him.

"Diamond, why are you doing this?"

"Doing what?" Remo took two steps back from Diamond. Diamond let out a light laugh.

"How are you supposed to protect me, when you won't even let me get close to you?"

"Because I'm trying to control myself, I'm not going to play with the pussy."

"Good, because I don't play with the dick." Diamond walked up to Remo and licked his lips.

"I remember you use to be with Gunna on Smith Street all the time"

"He was fun for the moment, and Tee tried my gangster one night and here I am now."

"So, why you trying me?"

"Because of how you looked at me all them times."

"Back then and just like now, you are forbidden fruit. Yeah, I like to look but I know I can't touch."

"It sounds like to me, you are afraid to eat the fruit off the forbidden tree. Take a bite and I might be able to open your third eye." Diamond looked at Remo in a seductive way and walked up closer to him. "What's up, Remo, you afraid to take a risk?"

"No, but I'm not going to be corrupted by your disloyalty, no matter how good you look." Remo looked at Diamond and walked outside to the back of the house to smoke a blunt.

***

"Dapp, ride through the Flat Tops, to see if we can see these fools." Dapp nodded and pulled his gun out and placed it on his lap.

"These fools ain't crazy. They not posted on the block."

"You never know Dapp, they might have built their nuts up and decided to come to the playground."

"Niggas don't know they are about to be in the belly of the beast, if they are out here." Dapp rode down Prospect Street and pulled over when he saw a few people posted up in front of the white house. He and Tee got out the car and walked up to them.

"What's the word on the block, my guys?

"Shit, we just out here, Tee. Posted up, watching the scene."

"I see y'all, but where is that fool Gunna at?"

"Them niggas be posted up on the next block in the green house on the dead-end."

"They over there now?"

"I don't even know, homie, them dudes be so ducked off in the cut."

"I feel you, homie, them niggas know what time it is."

"The block already been talking about that shit."

"Ya, stay up. Come on, Dapp, we out." Once back in the car, Dapp looked at Tee.

"What you trying to do, big homie?"

"Let's go see this house they was talking about."

"Cool." Dapp pulled up on the dead-end street two houses down from the green house.

"I guess we know where they be at now, so what's the move?"

"We are going to strip up and come back tonight. Come on, let's go get this bitch her food, and get ready for tonight."

"We are going to air this bitch out. I can't wait to see this nigga dead body in a fucking casket." Tee looked at Dapp as he pulled off.

***

"Munchie, come check this out." Munchie walked to the living room window and looked out and saw Tee and Dapp pulling off.

"Them fools don't even know. They think they are the hunters when they just the prey. I told you sooner or later, they will come asking questions, that's why I had them young homies on the block. I blessed them with an ounce of dope, just to tell Dapp or Tee where we be at, now when they come back tonight, we are going to roll they ass."

"Fucking right." Gunna watched Munchie walk off.

SAYNOMORE

Chapter 24

Jake opened the back doors to the detail shop and saw a gift-wrapped box sitting at the back door. He looked around to see was anybody was out there, then picked up the box, he knew what was inside it already. He locked the back door, bringing the box to Manny's office. Manny looked at him when he walked in with the box.

"So, she sent us the head, I was wondering when she was going to send the head to us. She's showing us she can turn into the heartless cartel bitch that Omar made her into. Open the box and let's see if she left us a note inside." Jake opened the box and looked at the head in a clear plastic bag, with a note on top of the plastic bag. Jake pulled the note out of the box and passed it to, Manny.

Manny read the note out loud, "Let this be the first of my body count. And it will stop when your head is in a plastic bag on Big Country steps. Manny, you fucked with the wrong bitch." There was a kiss on the paper in red lipstick.

"Look, Jake. I guess this is the kiss of death." Jake smiled.

"She left her mark for you to see."

"Yeah, she did. Get this out of here and kill the bitch."

"that's already being taken care off."

***

Ice-Berg looked at Carmen as she rolled the blunt up at the kitchen table. He poured them two shots of brandy Carmen was beautiful, five-nine with light skin and light brown eyes. Her hair was long and curly, it was honey blonde. She had a small waist that matched the rest of her body. Carmen could be a reflection of the black J-Lo. She hard an hourglass body that was a showstopper, and a smile to die for.

"What's good with that blunt, lil mama?"

"It's already rolled, I'm waiting for you to come with the shots."

"I'm on my way to you now trust and believe that."

Carmen picked up the blunt and lit it, blowing the smoke out of her mouth, looking at Ice-Berg.

"Let me smoke with you, baby girl, pass me the blunt."

Carmen passed Ice-Berg the blunt, as she took her shot of brandy. "So, what made you reach out to me, Ice-Berg?"

"Real shit, you fly as fuck and I wanted to get to know you"

"So, what you want to know about me, Ice-Berg?"

"I ain't never seen you in the dance before, so where you from?"

"I'm from the Ville, the north side. What you know about that?"

"I know a little something about Amityville, so you came to crime dance just to see the b-ball game?"

"Yes, I did. Wyandanch be piped up... it be lit out here."

"So, who you was out here with?"

"By my fucking self. I do not like bitches at all."

"Dead ass, I know how you feel, that's why i don't fuck with niggas."

"So, who you get money with then?"

"My day-one."

"Tell me this, Ice-Berg. You get money, you got a fly ass spot, where's the bitch at in your life?"

"I could ask you the same thing. You have a banging ass body, you can dress your ass off, so where is your dude at?"

"I don't have dudes, I have friends."

"That's how you living?"

"You never answered my question, Ice-Berg"

"I have a friend I'm fucking, but that's all, we ain't on no booed-up shit."

"So, you are a rolling stone?"

"No, I ain't no rolling stone, let's just say I live day by day"

"I guess we are alike in some ways."

"So, you trying to stay the night with me?"

"Nigga, you got me fucked up, what you think you can smoke a blunt with me, take a few shots of brandy, and going to jump on the dick? I'm not one of these trash dance bitches." Carmen looked at Ice-Berg and snapped her neck at him.

"Chill, baby girl. I didn't mean it like that, I'm just respecting the vibe we have."

"I hear you, nigga, but that weak ass game is not going to work with me." Ice-Berg looked at Carmen and laughed. That's when there was a knock at the door, Ice-Berg got up and opened the door, he smiled when Realz walked in.

"What's good, fam?"

"You know, pulling up, making sure everything's smooth before I hit the block for the night."

"I'm good, chilling with baby girl, just vibing."

"Yo that's a big fact. What's up, ma?"

"Hey, how you doing?"

"I'm doing good, beautiful, but check me out. Ice-Berg let me holla at you for a second." Ice-Berg walked Realz to the kitchen, away from Carmen.

"What it do, though?"

"You got a quarter bird on you? I'm trying to take it with me to the other side of town."

"Yeah, I got you. Post up for a minute let me go get that for you." Realz pulled out his phone and sent a text out.

"Here you go right here, fam."

"Damn, that was fast as fuck, bro"

"Shit, you don't know by now, I bag everything up in quarters."

"You know what, I wasn't even thinking. Like, I got so much shit on my mind right now."

"What the fuck you got going on?"

"Trying to take over a new trap."

"Where at?"

"Bay Shore, my mans out there told me it's a gold mine, so I'm trying to get me some of them rubies and diamonds out there."

"Copy that, let me know if you need me to pull up."

"Say less, I got you, but from what I seen when I first walked into the door, it looks like you have your hands full."

"Shit, I'm trying to have them full up."

"Ice-Berg gave Realz a pound, before he walked out the kitchen to the living room.

"Baby girl, take it easy. I'm out."

"You too, nice meeting you."

"Likewise." Ice-Berg closed and locked the door after Realz walked out.

"Now beautiful, where was we at?"

"With you trying to run some weak ass game, trying to taste my honey pot." Ice-Berg laughed.

"Carmen, you are too much for TV. I know all the females from the Ville can't be like this."

No, no, no. I'm the last of a dying breed."

"Come on, let's go for a ride."

"Where to?"

"To get something to eat."

"I guess."

"Whatever, girl, come on." Carmen put her glass down and got up and walked to the door with Ice-Berg.

Chapter 25

Tee looked at Dapp, Remo and Solo, as he walked into his backyard. "Yo, y'all know the drill, shoot or get shot. Remo, I want you to set the house on fire. Solo, you light that bitch up, and me and Dapp is going to stand on the side of the street ducked off, and whoever run out that house, we are going to wet them up." Dapp looked at Tee.

"Come on, let's go handle the business. I'm tired of these bitch ass niggas breathing the same air as me."

"Come on, y'all, let's ride the fuck out." Everyone got into Tee's truck, as Tee lit up a blunt and played 50 Cent's "Many Men" as they rode out.

***

Munchie and Gunna sat in the abandoned house across the street, watching out the window for Tee and Dapp to pull up.

"Munchie, how you think these fools are going to pull up?"

"Nine out of ten times, they are going to be on some drive-by shit, so when they pull up and start letting off, we are going to fire they ass up."

"You know how I get down… my name is Gunna for a reason. I'm trying to put a hole in a nigga face tonight."

"Say less, just be on point."

***

Tee pulled the truck over before he entered the Flat Tops and turned the music off.

"Tee, what's good, why you pull over?"

"Dapp, something don't feel right, them little niggas gave up that information way too quick, and everybody knows we got smoke with them boys."

"So, you think they are setting us up?"

"I think they was paid to tell us where they be at, and you said you pulled up on Don-don and asked where this nigga lay his head at. I'm willing to bet he called Munchie and told him the business and put him on point. You know what, let's go find this nigga Don-don and see what he got in his phone, and if he put Munchie up on game, he's going to be put in a black bag tonight."

"We might be able to find that nigga at the Pinks, that's where he be trapping at."

"That's where we are headed at then."

"Solo?"

"what's good, Dapp?"

"Roll his ass if he's lying"

Tee pulled up to the Pinks store and parked the truck as they looked at Don-don.

"Y'all niggas go handle your business."

"Solo, remember what I said. Come on y'all." Tee watched as Dapp, Remo and Solo walked up to Don-don. Dapp pulled his gun out.

"Where the fuck is your phone at, nigga?" Don-don looked at all three of them.

"Dapp, why the fuck you keep fucking with me?"

"Nigga, this ain't twenty-one questions, you heard what the fuck I said. Where the fuck is your phone at?" Don-don looked at Dapp, then Remo, and punched Dapp in the face knocking him back some and took off running. Solo pulled his .45 caliber out and shot Don-don two times in the back, dropping him. Don-don fell on the ground and Solo ran up to him, with Dapp and Remo.

"You, bitch ass motherfucker, you took blood out of my lip."

"Come on, Dapp, don't do this shit not like this, homie."

"I ain't your homie, Munchie your homie, ya bitch ass nigga." Dapp nodded at Solo, and Solo walked up to Don-don, pulled his gun out and shot him dead in the forehead. All of them ran back to Tee's truck and he pulled off.

"Now that's how the fuck you handle the business. When we ride through the Flat Tops, y'all fools drop the windows down and clap them niggas who tried to set us up."

"Copy that, it's murder in the Ville tonight," Dapp said.

Tee cut down Smith Street, headed to the Flat Tops, Remo rolled down the window and pulled himself out of it. As he held on to the handle on the inside of the truck celling, Solo passed him the MAC-11. Dapp had his window down, so did Solo. Tee cut off the lights to the truck and floored it towards the niggas on the block. All that was heard was gunshots, it sounded like World War 3 in the hood, sparks fired from the guns lighting the night up. Tee pulled over and jumped out of the truck, ran up on the dude who told him where Munchie was at, on the ground bleeding.

"Pussy nigga, you tried to set me the fuck up, now look at you." Tee shot him three times in the face, then he ran back to his truck and pulled off. They left three dead bodies out there in the Flat Tops.

***

Gunna was looking out the window, as Tee pulled up. He yelled for Munchie.

"Yo Munchie, Tee and them is spraying the block up, they hitting up the little homies." Gunna and Munchie ran out the door, guns in hands, they ran on the block. "Damn, Munchie, they killed the little homies." Munchie looked at the three homies dead on the block.

"Come on, Gunna. We got to get the fuck out of here before them boys come."

SAYNOMORE

Chapter 26

Pillz opened his eyes and looked around the hospital room. He had IVs in his arm, and his body was sore to the touch, he thought back to the day he was shot. Whoever shot him thought he was dead. He looked to the right, and saw the picture of him, Monay and Promise, A few minutes went by, and a nurse walked into the room.

"Good afternoon, Mr. Kent. I'm glad to see you are up, how long have you been up for?"

"I don't know, ten maybe fifteen minutes, how long have I been here for?"

"Today makes three days, you came in pretty banged up. For a while, we wasn't sure if you were going to make it."

"How many times was I shot?"

"Six in total, you are very lucky to be here still. Let me go get the doctor for you, I'll be back shortly." Pillz closed his eyes as he replayed the day he was shot.

Pillz couldn't believe how he was caught slipping again, this is the second time he got caught down bad, he knew there was an angel watching over him, because he beat death twice. He opened his eyes when he heard the room door open, and saw the doctor and the nurse walk back in.

"Mr. Kent, I see you are up, how do you feel?"

"Like I've been beaten over and over again."

"Well, you were in bad shape when you came in. I didn't think you were going to make it."

"How long before I can be discharged?"

"I want to keep you around for a few more days, three at the most." Pillz laid his head back own and closed his eyes.

"Ok, that's fine with me, Doctor."

"Good, now everything on your chart looks good. I'm let you rest, and I will see you tomorrow." The nurse and the doctor walked out the room. Pillz closed his eyes and went back to his thoughts.

***

"Hey, Detective Moorehouse, do you think there is some kind of connection between our victim who is missing his head, and Mr. Kent who was shot six times in an attempt to kill him?"

"You know what, Detective Stone, there might just be one. First, Kent got shot six times and the driver was in a van. Not even a week goes by and the same van, in just a different color... the white driver gets his head chopped off."

"So, you thinking whoever shot Kent, made Kent's people come back out of retaliation and killed the driver of the van?"

"You hit it on the head, Moorehouse."

"So, it's time to look deeper into Mr. Kent's record."

"Yeah, but I hear over the radio we have a 187 at the Pinks on 110, and that there are three 187's in the Flat Tops on Prospect Street. From what I heard, it was a drive-by."

"Come on, Stone, let's go see the mess out there"

"After you, Moorehouse."

***

Tee watched as the truck was in flames, he looked at Dapp, Remo and Solo, he called them all over to him.

"Listen up y'all, there is going to be a lot of heat on us we all caught bodies tonight. No gun no case, so pass me y'all burners but first, wipe them bitches down, take the clips out and do the same thing to them. We are leaving them here with the truck. So, wipe them down good." Tee watched as everyone wiped the guns off and threw them in the fire.

"Come on, y'all, let's get the fuck up out of here." They all walked to Tee's BMW and got in, as Tee pulled off.

Chapter 27

Manny sat quietly as he listened to Big Country on the phone, he leaned back in his chair as he smoked his cigar.

"Manny what I don't understand is, why would Jake have this Pillz person shot up, and then go after Monay? Monay is a heartless, cold-hearted bitch, she is a true killer from the heart."

"I know who she is, sir, I have been around her for many years."

"Just because you are around a person don't mean you know them. Let me ask you this, do you remember the 1991 Catholic Church massacre, where the priest was gutted open like a fish? His body was hanging from the ceiling with a pool of blood under him, and twenty-one members of the Catholic Church were killed, everyone with their throats cut from ear to ear."

"Yeah, I remember that year and how the people was killed."

"To this day, Manny, it is still an unsolved case, but let me let you in on something. Monay was a priest that day, the wine offering was passed out. As they drank the blood of Jesus Christ, she poisoned everyone that day and then took her knife, walked up to each member of the church and cut their throats. And what she did to the priest, the Man of God, there is a spot in hell's fire picked out for her. She's coming for you, Manny, and I hope you are ready to bury this bitch, because she's not going to stop till she kills you. Remember she is whoever she needs to be… a lover, a priest, a warrior, that's how Omar made her, and that is who she is."

"Don't worry, I will be sending you her head real soon."

"I hope it's not your head in the box when I open it."

Big Country hung up the phone. Manny put the phone on the hook and finished smoking his cigar, as he looked out the window as it rained.

***

"Munchie, we got to pull up tonight. We got four homies in black bags, niggas is dropping like flies, while we in the cut like a Band-Aid." Munchie was smoking a cigarette, listening to Gunna talk as he cleaned his gun.

"I know where Tee rest his head at, so we are going to roll that nigga tonight."

"Man, fuck rolling him tonight. It's raining right now, it's dark as hell outside right now, we need to pull up now. He ain't going to think or be expecting us." Munchie put his cigarette out and tucked his gun into his waist.

"Come on then, let's ride out."

"That's what the fuck I'm talking about."

***

"Diamond, come here beautiful." Tee watched as Diamond walked up to him. She sat down next to him on the bed.

"What's up, baby?" Tee placed his hand on Diamond's lap.

"You feel like going to the store?"

"Sure, what you want me to get?"

"Some blunts, and two beef patties with cheese."

"Sure, I'ma go get it now, bae." Diamond got up and walked out the house, got into Tee's car and was driving off when she got a text message to her phone.

She smiled and turned around and pulled Tee's car back into the yard, walked into the house and placed the car keys down on the counter. Tee came out the room.

"You ain't taking the car?"

"No, I don't want nobody to see the car and think it's you and shoot up the car. I'm just going to walk, bae."

"Cool, I understand. You a gun slinger." Tee walked up to Diamond and kissed her forehead before she walked back out the door. Once outside, Diamond pulled back out her phone, and sent a text out. A few seconds later, a white Benz picked her up off Albany Avenue. Diamond got into the car

"Damn, baby girl, you look good as fuck."

"I do, Tye?"

"Yeah, you do, and I'm willing to bet you taste better then you look."

"You keep talking like that, you going to have a wet spot on the seat of your Mercedes Benz." Tye started laughing.

"Is that right?"

"Yes, it is. When did you get back in town?"

"Last night, around 10:00 pm, but I have to go back out of town tomorrow night, to do another show in DC, and then I'm flying to Florida."

"I see you, Tye, doing big things."

"So, you busy?"

"No, I have some time to kill."

"Good, let's go for a ride, bae."

***

Tee heard a knock at the door, he got his gun and walked to the front door. "Who is it?"

"Rude-Boy and J.D." Tee opened up the door to let them in the house.

"What's popping, homies?"

"Shit, we came to buy some of that gas off you."

"That's why y'all niggas is out here in the rain?"

"Fucking right, niggas is trying to get high, fam."

"Hold up, let me go get it from the back." Tee walked to the back room, while Rude-Boy and J.D. waited for him in the front room.

Munchie and Gunna were outside Tee's back door, looking at Rude-Boy and JD through the window, standing in Tee's living room. Munchie nodded at Gunna. A second later, Gunna aimed his gun through the window and blasted. JD stumbled back and dropped to the floor. Munchie got Rude-Boy with successive shots that dropped him too. They kicked the door open and ran inside.

Gunna ran up to JD as he was laying on the ground and blew his face off. Tee grabbed his gun and cocked it back, he was leaning against the doorframe of his room, Munchie shot Rude-Boy two more times in the face and pointed at the back room. Gunna nodded and started walking that way.

"Y'all coming in my fucking house, both ya bitch ass mother-fuckers is dead."

"Yeah, just like your two homies in the living room on the floor in a pool of blood. Don't worry, we are on our way back there to you now." Tee came around the corner of the door, firing shots at Munchie and Gunna. Gunna pointed his pump at the side of the wall and let off four rounds. When Gunna stepped back, Munchie started shooting through the wall. Tee dropped his gun when he got shot in the shoulder. He looked out the window, and then at his gun on the floor. Tee shook his head and ran to the window, jumping out of it. Gunna ran to the back room and saw Tee running through the yard.

"He's running through the backyard... he climbed out the window." Munchie took off running through the house out the back door, he saw Tee hopping the gate and started shooting at him, then he ran back in the house. Gunna met him in the living room.

"Come on, let's get the fuck up out of here before the police come, Gunna."

"Come on, we out." Gunna and Munchie ran out of Tee's house back to their car and drove off. Munchie took off his face mask and looked at Gunna.

"That's how you lay a motherfucker down."

"Fucking right."

Tee fell out in his homie's backyard, a few houses down from his house, out of breath and loss of blood.

Chapter 28

Diamond had her legs open as Tye was deep inside her, and her head was hanging off the bed as Tye's home boy had his manhood in her mouth. Diamond had spit coming out her mouth as he pumped in and out, touching the back of her throat. Diamond was trying to push Tye back some because he was deep inside her stomach. Tye pulled out and looked at his home boy, who started jacking off in Diamond's mouth to cum inside of it. Diamond Got up and stuck out her tongue to show him the cum on her tongue before she swallowed it, while Tye put her in the doggy style, as he went back inside of her.

"Damn bae, I can't take this dick, please pull out some, please."

"Chill baby, I got you, just chill." Tye pulled out of Diamond as she laid flat on the bed catching her breath, Tye put some KY-Jelly on his stick and pulled Diamond up by her waist. Without saying anything, Tye rammed himself into Diamond's ass. She let out a loud cry.

"Baby, please take it out, please."

"No, you are going to take all of this dick, baby."

"Baby, you are ripping me open, it's too big."

Tye didn't pay Diamond no mind as he continued to go deeper into her. Diamond started to shake and as her body fell flat on the bed, Tye stayed over top of her in the frog style. When he pulled out, his homie went right in. They fucked Diamond nonstop for two hours. Diamond was now laying on the bed with her knees to her chest, while Tye sat in the chair rolling up a blunt as he looked at Diamond

"Diamond, I swear you got the best pussy in the world."

"Real shit, and baby girl, your head game is on point. I'm thinking about getting round two of that good-good."

"Y'all got my stomach hurting fucking me like that. You two big dick niggas, y'all can't fuck me no more but I'll suck y'all dicks if you want before you leave."

"After we smoke, bae, come hit this blunt." Diamond couldn't believe she was just fucking two major rap artists from Murder Inc. and got pictures with them. She felt when they were cumming inside of her, both of them more than two times when she was riding them, back-to-back. She knew what she was doing and in nine months, she was going to have her baby boy or girl. She wasn't worried about Tee, he never came in her, plus they used condoms all the time.

***

When Tee opened his eyes, he was in the back of the ambulance, he heard people talking as he was going in and out.

"Sir, can you hear me? Blink your eyes if you hear me."

Tee blinked his eyes two times, before they rolled to the back of his head, and he passed out again.

"We're losing him, we are losing him, I need some help over here now."

***

Dapp and Remo walked up to the crowd of people, all outside Tee's house looking at the scene. There were over twenty-one police officers out there, the road was blocked off and yellow caution tape was around Tee's house.

"Yo, what the fuck happened out here?" Dapp was waiting on Tory to let him know what went down.

"Niggas kicked in Tee's door and bodied Rude-Boy and J.D., and word is Tee being rushed to the hospital, they found the homie clapped up behind Willie's spot." Dapp looked at Remo and patted him on the chest two times.

"Let's get the fuck up out of here."

"Where we headed?"

"To kill a fake gangster and i know where to find him at."

***

Monay walked around the empty house. It took her three days to pack it up with the help of the movers, everything was on two 18-wheelers on the way to L.A. the only thing she kept was her black BMW. She knew Manny had cop friends, she needed to find out who they were, she was going to show Manny the demon Omar made. She walked out her house and drove to J's Bar. She stepped out the car wearing all black, she had two fully loaded black 9mm on her. Monay walked into the bar, took a seat at the back table and looked around till a waiter walked up to her.

"Hey what can I Get for you?"

"A Long Island iced tea and a blue motherfucker."

"Coming right up."

One of the officers made eye contact with Monay, he picked his beer up and walked to her table and sat down. He took a sip of his beer and looked around. "I ain't know dead females enjoyed a drink."

"You're only dead when you stop breathing. I didn't know Manny had you on his payroll." Before the officer could say a word, the waiter brought Monay her drinks.

"There you are, call me if you need another."

"I will, thank you."

"Take your shots so we can leave, you have an appointment with someone." Monay picked up the shot of blue motherfucker and took it, then she chased it with the Long Island iced tea.

"See, one thing Manny shoulda told you about me, I'm the wrong bitch to fuck with."

"Come the fuck on, now." Monay looked dead in the officer's eyes and got up. When he turned his head, Monay already had her gun pointed at it. Everyone in the bar looked when they heard the sound of the gun going off and the officer's head being blown off, Monay looked on as everyone looked at her with both guns in her hands, as she made her way to the door.

"Please don't fuck up and die, if you try and stop me, a lot more bodies are going to drop."

"Put the guns down, you have no wins, you are not walking out of here alive." Monay looked at the gun pointed at her a few feet from her and the officers talking to her.

"You might be right, let's see who is a better shot." Monay dropped down to her knees and let off three shots to the officer's chest, dropping him. She got up and ran behind the bar as she was getting shot at, she looked up and started shooting out all the lights in the bar. Someone jumped over the bar and grabbed her from behind, picked her up and slammed her on her back. Monay pointed both guns at him and started shooting him in the chest. He fell backwards on the floor.

She got up, shooting at everyone she saw, she ran till a shotgun blew out the glass from the bar door. She turned around and shot the bartender in the face, dropping her. Then she opened the bar doors, ran to her car and drove off as officers ran out the bar shooting at her car. Monay made a right on a dead-end block and got out the black car she stole and set it on fire. she got into her BMW and drove off.

Chapter 29

A nurse pushed Pillz to the front of the hospital in a wheelchair to facilitate his release. After pushing himself up from the wheelchair and thanking the nurse, Pillz turned his phone on and had twenty-six missed calls and sixteen voice messages. He called Monay, after a few rings she picked up.

"Baby, you are up. I was just on my way back up there to see you."

"Yeah, I been up for three days now, waiting on you."

"Look bae, we are not going to talk over the phone, I'm on my way now to see you."

"I'm out front, waiting on you to pick me up."

"I'll be there in twenty minutes, bae."

"Cool, I'm here waiting." Pillz hung up the phone and called Munchie, who picked up right away.

"What the fuck, where you been, homie?"

"I been in ICU for the last two weeks, my body is fucked up, I can't even really move like that, homie."

"Why the fuck was you in ICU?"

"Someone caught me at the light and aired me the fuck out. I just knew I was dead, son fucked me over bad as hell."

"On the gang, I ain't know that shit, you was M.I.A. I ain't know what to think, but we need to talk face-to-face like yesterday, can you pull up on me?"

"Yeah, wifey picking me up now, so I'll be there in a minute."

"Copy that." Pillz hung up the phone as Monay was pulling up, he opened up the car door and got inside. Monay leaned over and gave him a kiss on the lips before pulling off.

"How you feeling, bae?"

"Fucked up. Niggas tried to take my life, they had me down bad, I ain't even see it coming."

"Bae, it was Manny who tried to have you killed, you wasn't going to see it coming. These ain't no street niggas, we are dealing with the cartel, and it's not going to stop."

"So how the fuck are we going to get out of this?"

"We have to kill Manny and Jake and that's just the first step."

"Take me to the house, I need to take a hot bath, before I go see Munchie."

"Baby, there is nothing at the house. It's empty, the cars and everything is gone, it's on the way to the new house. Let's go see Munchie and after that, I will take you to the rental spot till we leave New York." Pillz closed his eyes as he leaned back in the car.

"Who Got Promise?"

"The babysitter, they are at the new house."

"You remember where Munchie stay?"

"Yeah, I do." Pillz pulled out his phone and called Munchie, after a few calls he picked up.

"Yo, yo."

"I'm on my way to your spot now, I'll be there in ten minutes, homie."

"Oh shit, I forgot to tell you. I'm not over there no more, let me text you the new address real quick."

"Man, hurry up because I'm ready to go to my spot."

"Copy that." Pillz got the text with the address to Munchie's new spot, he showed Monay. Within twenty minutes they were pulling up in his driveway. Pillz and Monay got out the car and walked to the front door, Pillz was walking with a cane. Munchie opened the front door for them to come inside.

"My nigga and the black queen, come in." Pillz walked to the kitchen table and took a seat.

"What the fuck is going on, Munchie?"

"Shit is wicked out here right now, bodies is dropping left and right."

"What you mean? What the fuck ain't you telling me?" Monay looked at Munchie and watched how he was moving.

"Look, the nigga Dapp came blasting, him and Tee like two nights ago. Since this shit been happening between the two of us, we lost five soldiers. But last night we pulled up on Tee and kicked his door and bodied two niggas he had posted up with him and clapped his ass." Munchie sat down at the table with them and started rolling up a blunt.

"Munchie, you know Tee not going to stop until you are in a black bag, and where is Dapp at?"

"Shit, I don't know, I just know shoot on sight." A few minutes passed and Gunna walked in the door.

"Oh shit. The real Pillz Berry, what the fuck is rocking, my guy?"

"Shit, we rocking." Gunna walked up to Pillz and gave him a pound."

"Damn, big homie, last time I seen you, you was good. Now you are walking around with a cane, what the fuck happened to you?"

"Motherfuckers is trying to stop my heart from pumping but I'm good, homie. Munchie was just telling me about what's been going down in the hood."

"Big facts, niggas put that hot steel in that nigga's life."

"Let's talk about the money." Munchie looked at Pillz.

"Shit, we good on that tip."

"Good, let me get that then."

Munchie got up from the table and walked to the back room. He came back a few minutes later with a book bag filled with money, he placed it on the table.

"That's a hundred and twenty grand on the head." Pillz passed the bag to Monay.

"Look let me go make my other rounds and I'll be back tomorrow night to see you."

"Copy that, that's cool with me." Monay picked up the bag and walked out the house behind Pillz, once in the car she looked at Pillz.

"Baby, we are riding around picking up crumbs, let the birds have them."

"I want everything my blood spilled on the block for. Can you take me to the rental spot now?"

"Yeah, sure."

***

"What the fuck went down with you and Baby Girl?"

"Man, that shit was a dead end. Realz, the cookie jar was close and locked down."

"Damn, baby was bad as fuck, I woulda paid for her to open that cookie jar."

"Man, I pulled out stacks on this Bitch, over a hundred thousand bands, took her for a ride in the whip and all."

"Damn… a hundred thousand bands and took her for a ride in the Benz, and you still ain't get the pussy. I told you… you only have a face a mother could love. You need to face the fact you ugly as fuck."

"Nigga, fuck you… on gang, I get pussy."

"I know you do, but what are we going to do? We are running low on work."

"Shit, I'm waiting on Pillz to hit me back now, Realz."

"Shit, we might need to take a ride to the Ville."

Man, they got a body count out there like they are at war in the Middle East. I'm good on that shit."

"Shit, what's the move for tonight?'

"Man, I'm in the cut till this nigga Pillz hit my jack back."

"Cool, I'm out. Let me know the move, hit my line when you are ready or you got the re-up."

"I got you, homie." Ice-Berg walked Realz to the front door, and locked it behind him. He then walked into his bedroom and looked at Candy on the bed, she smiled and sat up and looked at him.

"Is he gone?"

"Yeah, I just walked him to the front door."

"So, where was we at?"

"I think you was about to show me how strong your mouth game was."

"How do it feel knowing you are fucking your right-hand man's wife?"

"We ain't fucking, you are sucking my dick."

"I hate you but love how real you are so much."

"I know you do, now come here, sexy." Candy walked up to Ice-Berg and dropped on her knees.

Realz walked around Ice-Berg's house, he had to take a piss. As he was pissing on the side of the house, he looked through Ice-Berg's window, and saw his wife sucking his dick. Realz pulled his gun out and walked to the front door, knocked two times.

"Damn baby, hold on, someone is at the door."

"Let them knock, I don't want to stop."

"Chill, it might be Pillz, baby girl." Ice-Berg pulled up his pants and walked to the front door and opened it.

"What's up, homie?"

"What the fuck you mean, what's up?"

"You fucking Candy, you foul ass nigga?"

"Yo, you tripping, nigga."

"I might be, and I might not be." Realz pointed his gun at Ice-Berg and shot him two times in the chest. Ice-Berg fell on the ground and looked at Realz, with blood coming out of his mouth.

"Realz, you shot me."

"No, pussy, I killed you." Realz shot Ice-Berg in the face two times and walked in the back room, where Candy was in the corner of the room crying.

"Realz, please don't, please." Realz looked at Candy and shot her two times in the head. He walked to Ice-Berg's closet, pulled out the duffle bags with the last of the work and money, and walked out the house.

SAYNOMORE

Chapter 30

Manny sat back, smoking a cigar, watching the news reporter talking about the killings in J's Bar. Jake sat quietly in Manny's office listening to what they were talking about.

"We are here at J's Bar, off of Sunrise Highway where there was a mass shooting, three off-duty police officers were killed. We have a witness who said she saw everything. Ms. Wright, can you tell me what you saw?"

"Yes, I work here, and a black female came in the bar wearing all black, she sat at the back table. She ordered two drinks then one of the regulars here, an officer, walked to her table. They sat down and a few seconds later, I bring her drinks. Then they both stood up, and that's when I heard the gunshot, and I saw Officer Malone laying there on the floor shot.

"Then the female yelled, 'No one else has to die.' She pointed guns at everyone, she was trying to make it out the door. When one of the other officers told her she wasn't going to leave alive, the next thing you know, she dropped down to her knees and started shooting. She shot the lights out and before you knew it, it was three more dead bodies. She only shot at the officers who was shooting at her. She was gone as fast as she came in."

"Thank you, Ms. Wright, there you have it from one of the employees here at J's Bar."

Manny looked at Jake. "She know what she is doing."

"You know Malone was on our payroll. He knew who was, she was hoping he would recognize her and he did, and it cost him his life. So, where do we go from here?"

"We wait for her to come to us." Manny put the cigar down and got up and fixed his tie.

"Come on, Jake, we have to meet someone."

***

"Moorehouse, what you think about this?" Detective Moorehouse looked around the bar at the dead officers under the white sheets.

"The way Ms. Wright said she was moving she sounds like a professional. Thing about this, she came into a cop bar and killed three officers and made it out alive. She shot out the lights so she could shoot in the dark. I think she's cleaning up all loose strings, and I'm willing to bet the officer who walked to her table knew who she was. She came here to kill him, and whoever stood in her way. Now that makes me think we are dealing with the cartel and there is a war going on, on our streets, that's why so many people being killed."

"You make a good fucking point. I think we need to pay Mr. Kent another visit and find out why the cartel want him dead."

"Let's go do that now."

***

Pillz walked into the condo and laid down on the bed. Monay laid down next to him and was looking in his eyes.

"Tell me, Monay, what did you do?"

"I killed the man who shot you and cut off his head and I sent it to him, then the cop who pulled you over, I killed him and two other officers, the day before you got out the hospital."

"Monay, I love you, and you was right. We just need to leave this life behind us before one of us is in a black bag."

"I'm ready to leave now, tonight."

"We can't just yet, I have to drop two more off to Munchie first."

"There's nothing else out here, everything is on its way to the new house." Pillz got up and looked at Monay.

"Cool, we can leave tonight. I just have one more run to make."

"Good, I'm coming with you, so after your run we can just leave."

"Come on, let's go then." Monay drove Pillz downtown in the village, to a white house. Pillz pulled his phone out opened the car door and walked up to Carmen.

"Did you do what I asked you to do?"

"Yeah, I did"

"How do you feel about him?"

"He's a free lick."

"Good, I have something for you." Pillz handed Carmen the bag he had in his hand. It's a hundred and twenty bands in that bag. Kill both of them, do you think you can do that?"

"I'll call you in a few days."

"Ok." Pillz walked back to the car and got inside and looked at Monay.

"Come on, baby, let's go home."

"Pillz, who is she?"

"The bitch who is going to clean up my last two problems." Monay looked at Pillz and drove off.

SAYNOMORE

Chapter 31

Diamond sat on the side of Tee's bed while he was asleep, he's been in the hospital for two days. She rubbed his hand and turned his head to look at her and smiled.

"How long have I been here for?"

"Just two days, when I got back to your house, police was everywhere."

"Thank you for being here for me, bae."

"You know I love you." Diamond got up and kissed Tee on the mouth. "Let me go get the nurse for you, bae."

"Ok."

After Tee talked to the doctor, Diamond went to get him something to drink and eat.

"Diamond, I need my phone, can you get it for me?"

"Yeah, I'll get it now, bae." Diamond got up and handed Tee his phone. Tee called Dapp, after a few rings he picked up.

"Playboy, what the fuck? I'm glad you are still breathing."

"Come on, man... that shit was ugly, but it's going to take more than two niggas to put me down."

"Come on, big dog shit. I already know, so where you at now?"

"I'm still laid up in the hospital, I'm trying to check out this shit now."

"Facts, so you going back to the same spot?"

"Fuck no, that shit is a dub, I got another spot I'ma post up at off of Bayview."

"Shit, clap my jack when you ready for me to pick you up."

"Copy that, but I was just calling to let you know I was good."

"I already know you was going to walk through that shit like Desert Storm, hands down."

"Yo... love, homie."

"Love, my nigga." Tee hung up the phone and put his food tray on his lap and started to eat.

***

Carmen pulled up on Ice-Berg's street to see police every-where, the block was blocked off with yellow caution tape. An ambulance was parked outside his house with two EMH workers carrying a black body bag out of the house. She got out of her car and walked up to a crowd of people watching the scene.

"Excuse me, can you tell me what happened out here?"

"Ice-Berg and some female was killed, shot to death, they are just finding they bodies."

"Oh my God, do they know who did it?"

"No, nobody knows."

"This is just so sad, let me go."

"It is."

Carmen walked back to her car and got inside, and right before she was going to drive off, she saw Realz in the cut standing behind a tree, smoking a Newport watching the scene. She got back out of her car and walked up to him.

"Realz," she called out his name. Realz looked at Carmen.

"What's up, baby girl?"

"Nothing, I came out here to see Ice-Berg but I was just told he was killed."

"Yeah, dead ass, shit went really wrong for my homie and his people that was up in there with him."

"Do you know who did it?"

"Not yet."

"Damn, I'm about to leave, you need a ride somewhere?"

"Yeah, like ten minutes away from here."

"Come on, let's go, I don't mind." Realz walked to the car and got inside.

"You driving big baller style, I see."

"You can't gas my head up, it's just a Lexus, Realz"

"Yeah, you are right, the sports edition." All Carmen could do was laugh when Realz said that.

"Just like I told Ice-Berg, I'm not no jump-off bitch, money, cars, jewelry and shit like that do not impress me. I have my own."

"that's some real shit. I respect that hands down."

"So where is the female in your life?"

"She dead in my eyes."

"Damn, cold hearted, ain't you?"

"I stand on loyalty, and she was a disloyal bitch."

"We all stand on loyalty to somebody, Realz."

"Yeah, you right, but the motherfuckers you been loyal to, might not have been loyal to you."

"It sounds like someone you trusted betrayed you somehow."

"Yo, that's a whole true story, ma." Carmen nodded at Realz.

"The house to the right, you can drop me off at."

"Cool, you live here?"

"Yeah, this my spot."

"Ok, I see you."

"You should come by sometime."

"You know what, I might do that."

Carmen watched as Realz got out of the car. She drove back to Ice-Berg's house and as she got out, she overheard "Someone said they killed both of them, Ice-Berg and Realz' bitch."

"What was Realz' bitch doing over there?"

"You know how they used to rock." Carmen heard all she needed to hear to know Realz was the one who killed both of them. That's why he told her she was dead to him, and why he was stressing disloyalty. Carmen got back into her car and drove off, knowing she had to pay Realz a visit he wouldn't come back from.

***

Dapp sat on the hood of the car, smoking a blunt, waiting for Remo and Solo to pull up. When he saw Gunna drive past Smith Street, he jumped in his car and followed him to the Shell gas station, watched as Gunna went inside. He got out of his car, put his hoodie on and pulled his gun out. Gunna came walking out the gas station with his head down, packing his pack of Newport and drinking a soda when Dapp ran up on him.

"What's rocking, pussy nigga?" Gunna looked at Dapp as he pointed the gun at him.

"I'm supposed to be scared, nigga? My heart don't pump Kool-Aid for no fucking body, not even God, nigga."

"Well, tell him that when you see him, fuck boy." Dapp pulled the trigger, letting the bullets rip through Gunna's chest, blowing him back through the glass doors of the Shell gas station. Dapp ran up on him and shot him dead in the face, then ran to his car and pulled off before the police came to the scene. *Gunna had that shit coming in mo' ways than one. His heart don't got to pump Kool-Aid, but that bitch ain't pumping no mo'.*

Dapp pulled his car behind his home boy's house and pulled his phone out and called Remo to come pick him up. Dapp stayed in the cut till he saw Remo's car pulling up, then he ran and jumped in the back seat.

"Damn nigga why you moving like that?"

"Son, I just caught this nigga Gunna down bad and rolled his ass."

"Where the fuck at?"

"The Shell in the village. I popped his ass three times then I dome checked his ass."

"That's what the fuck I'm talking about, now we just got to catch this nigga Munchie slipping."

"Shit, his time is coming."

"Copy that, two times."

"Go to Solo spot, homie."

"Already."

Chapter 32

Munchie got a phone call, letting him know that Gunna was just killed at the Shell gas station in the village. He put his phone down and couldn't believe what he was hearing, his right-hand man just got bodied, they caught him slipping. Munchie got both of his guns and walked out the house to his car and drove off. Munchie put it on the hood that Gunna wasn't going to die alone tonight.

Munchie sat outside of South Shore Hospital. He pulled a Newport out of the box, dipped it in some angel dust, and lit it. he played Biggie Small and Jay Z's, "For The Love of The Dough," as he smoked the PCP. He looked around and got out the car and walked into the hospital up to the front desk.

"Hello, may I help you?"

"Yes, I'm here to see Marcus Toyal, can you tell me what floor he is on?"

"Sure, give me one moment and let me find him for you."

Munchie looked around the waiting room as he waited for the nurse to tell him what floor Tee was on, that's when he heard Diamond's voice. He looked and saw Tee and Diamond walking through the lobby doors. He pulled his gun out as the nurse let out a loud scream. Tee looked at Munchie as he held the gun in his hand.

"You see what the fuck is going on, nigga." Munchie let off two shots, shooting Tee and Diamond. Diamond fell backwards over some chairs. Tee hit the floor, as people were yelling and screaming, trying to get out the way. Munchie ran up to Tee as he was making it out the hospital door and shot him three times in the back. Tee fell flat on his back, he looked up at Munchie as blood was coming out of his mouth. Munchie didn't say a word, he stood over him, and shot him point blank in the head, killing him, blood went everywhere.

"Pussy nigga."

"Freeze, don't fucking move." Munchie looked and saw the police officer, point his gun at him. "Drop the fucking gun now, you have to the count of three." Munchie looked at the officer and turned around shooting, hitting the officer in the hand. He took off running through the parking lot, ducking down as he was running, as other police officers came running out the hospital shooting at him.

Munchie tripped and fell on the ground, went to get up and felt the shot to the side of his body. He fell back down on the ground he looked at the officer and shot him two times in the chest, Munchie went to get up when the blast from the shotgun took his breath away. Munchie rolled over and looked at the police officer pointing the gun at him.

"Don't do it, don't do it!" The officer looked into Munchie's eyes and knew what he was thinking. Munchie looked at the night sky as a tear rolled out his eye. He went to lift his arm up, that's when the officers started shooting Munchie multiple times in the upper part of the body, killing him. Munchie's arm fell back down, and his hand opened releasing the gun, as his head turned to the side. Blood dripped out of his mouth and his eyes closed.

Within the hour, the local news team was at the hospital, shooting live as the scene unfolded. "Breaking news... shooting at South Shore Hospital, leaving two dead and one police officer injured, and one female shot but the gunshot is not life threatening."

***

"Yo, yo... Dapp and Remo, come check this shit the fuck out, it went down at South Shore Hospital. The shit is being played all over the news right now." Dapp and Remo walked into Solo's living room and sat down on the couch and started watching the news. Dapp couldn't believe it when Tee's picture popped up on the screen as the victim who was killed, and then a few minutes later, Munchie's picture popped up on the screen as the gun man, who was shot and killed.

"Real shit, that pussy nigga snapped. Going to South Shore Hospital popping the bottle like that, Dapp." Dapp wasn't trying to hear what Remo was saying, his big homie just got rolled, that news just cut Dapp deep.

"Word musta got back to Munchie that Gunna got rocked to bed, and he said fuck it, and went up there on some Billy the Kid shit, bodied the homie and got himself killed."

Solo, you just said some real shit, and that's what probably happened too, I wouldn't put it past him." Dapp walked out the living room outside to the backyard and rolled a blunt up. He still was in shock, the man he called his brother, his homie, was dead because he couldn't catch a fuck nigga slipping. At that point in time, he just wanted to be left alone.

SAYNOMORE

Chapter 33

Carmen put on an all-black sweat suit with a pair of black Air Max. She put her hair in a ponytail and made sure her baby .38 was fully loaded. She got into her Lexus and drove to Realz' house. When she pulled up, it was 9:45 pm. She got out of her car and walked up to the door and knocked two times, she smiled when Realz opened the door and looked at her.

"What's up, beautiful? I'm glad you came by."

"Is that so?"

"Big facts, come in." Carmen smiled when Realz moved out the way for her to come into the house.

"You Got a nice spot up in here, Realz."

"Thanks, would you like something to drink? Ciróc, brandy, what's your choice?"

"I'll take Ciróc with two pieces of ice."

"Coming right up."

Carmen walked to the living room and sat down on the couch. "Oh, you was in here watching the game by yourself."

"Yeah, it's a lot better that way to me." Realz put Carmen's drink down on the table next to his and started to roll up a blunt.

"So, what brings you by tonight?" Carmen picked up her glass and took a sip, as Realz lit the blunt.

"I just really think we had a good vibe the other day, so I wanted to see for myself was I right or wrong."

"I felt the same thing, dead ass, baby Girl."

"That's what's up, can a bitch hit your blunt?" Realz laughed as he passed her the blunt.

"So, check me out, beautiful. There's no point in fake kicking it, you bad as fuck and I can tell you get money from your style, so what you do to get a check?"

"That's crazy, what type of question is that?" Carmen looked at Realz as she tilted her head.

"Shit, I'm just trying to see who I am around."

"I respect that. So, if you must know... I was in the military for six years, part of the Marine Corps, Forces Recon."

"So, you tough, like Barbie, huh?"

"I don't know about that, but I was specially trained to fight on land and sea."

"So, what happened, why ain't you still there?"

"Let's just say bigger opportunity came my way, and what I was doing for free, I get top dollar to do now. But enough about me, how you get your check?"

"Short story, straight to the point, I'm a dope boy."

"You sell weight?"

"Yeah, I do."

"Let me ask you, so what you get paid to do that you was doing for free before?" Carmen looked at Realz and took the last shot of her Ciróc.

"I get paid to kill people, Realz." Realz was lost for words. "Now let me ask you this, Realz, who is your supplier?"

"A friend of mine."

"So, if he was your friend as you say, why did you go behind his back and kill someone in Amityville on Smith Street, that started a hood-on-hood war?" Realz looked at Carmen and went to get up.

"Don't move, Realz, I want you to know you fucked up and crossed Pillz, that's why I'm here."

"You think I'ma let you kill me?"

"You're already dead." Carmen pulled her gun out and shot Realz three times, one to the stomach, one to the chest and the other one to his head. She looked at Realz' dead body and looked around his house, and she found the bag of money and cocaine. She took the cocaine out and poured it on the floor, she wiped her glass down and took the roach blunt with her and walked out of Realz' house. She got in her car and called Pillz, he picked up after two rings.

"Yo."

"It's done." Carmen hung up the phone and drove off.

***

Monay walked up to Pillz and wrapped her arms around his neck and looked into his eyes.

"Who was that on the phone, bae?"

"The last little bit of business in New York I had to take care of." Monay kissed Pillz on the lips

"Come on, dinner is ready, let's go eat."

"After you, bae."

As Pillz was walking into the kitchen, he stopped when he saw breaking news on the TV screen in the living room. He sat down in the living room on the couch, and was watching the news, he shook his head when he saw Munchie picture on the TV screen as the shooter, who was killed on the scene. Monay walked in the living room, holding Promise in her arms, she sat down next to Pillz as he watched the news.

"Baby, I know how close you are to Munchie, I'm sorry for your loss, baby."

"Thanks bae, what would make him go to the hospital on some blazing fire shit? He snapped." Before Monay could say a word, the news went to another scene that happened before the hospital shooting and showed the video of Gunna being killed at the Shell gas station.

"There is the answer to your question, why he snapped like that, he just couldn't take it no more."

"I see, so Dapp is the last nigga standing."

"Baby, what are you thinking?"

"I don't know, it's so much shit going on in the hood right now, three of my homies are dead right now."

"Bae, look at me. You don't need to go back out there right now. You know we are facing a much bigger problem. We don't need to open a door that we closed, there is nothing we can do for them, they are dead."

"I know that. Come on, bae, I don't want to see no More. I just want to eat dinner."

SAYNOMORE

Chapter 34

"Jake, what can you tell me about me about progress with Monay and this Pillz Character?"

"Nothing, I can't find them, not even the investigator. However, he did find an address, but he said the house was empty as if they just moved."

"She was smart enough to move, she knew we would find the house. She smart, she knows how to move, but somebody knows where she is, we just have to find that one person, to lead us to the bitch."

"He is working on that now, he said there was some mail in the house, one letter but it had a different name on it, so he is looking into that now."

"there's one thing I know, there is always a slip-up no matter what, now let's see what this address, have to do with Monay." Manny sat back in his chair and lit his cigar.

"Jake, make sure this investigator is working around the clock to we find this bitch."

"I'll get on the right now, sir." Jake got up and walked out of Manny's office, Manny picked up the phone and called an old friend of his, for a favor.

***

Brandy heard a knock at her door, she got up off the couch and walked to her front door. When she opened her door, she saw an older white male standing there holding a badge.

"Hello, my name is Cody White, and I'm looking for a Brandy Lawson. Is she home?' Brandy looked at the man and knew something wasn't right.

"She's not here, and what is this about?"

"It's a police matter, I am not at liberty to talk about it with you, and may I ask who you are?"

"I'm her friend, I'm watching the house for her until she comes back in town."

"Ok friend, do you have a name?" Brandy looked at the man standing on her doorstep. She knew something wasn't right with him.

"Yes, my name is Kira Long."

"Well, Ms. Long, do you know when Brandy would be back from out of town?"

"Sometime next week, do you have a card I can give her when she does come back?"

"Yeah, sure I do. Give me one second to pull it out." He handed Brandy the card.

"Thank you for your time and please make sure she gets the card."

"I will, have a good day, Mr. White."

"You too, Ms. Long." Brandy closed her house door and looked out the window, as Mr. White got in his car and drove off. She walked to her room and put her shoes on and walked out her front door, she got in her car and left. Mr. White watched from the corner of the street, as Brandy drove off.

He knew who she was already, he'd pulled her picture up, so he got out of his car and walked back down the street to her house. He walked around to the backyard and picked her lock to the back door and went inside. White looked around the house to see what he could find. He walked up stairs and saw a suitcase next to the dresser and opened it up. Inside, he saw a plane ticket from L.A. from a week ago, he closed the suitcase back up, placed the ticket in his pocket and left the house. Once he got in his car, he pulled his phone out and called Jake.

***

Brandy sat in her car in the mall parking lot and called Monay, after three rings she picked up.

"Hey beautiful, what's up?"

"Monay, a cop came to my house today looking for me, but he threw me off because he was by himself."

"What was his name?"

"Cody White, he gave me his card."

"What's the number on the card?"

"It's a 1-800 number, 1-800-555-0501."

"Ok, I got it how do he look?"

"He's about fifty-nine, white, dirty red hair, he put you in the mind of Carrot-Top."

"Listen to me, Brandy, do not go back home. They will be in your house waiting for you. Go to the other address in South Hampton, I have money in there, and I'm coming back to New York to get you. Brandy, do not go back to the house."

"Ok, I won't, I'm going to the other address now."

"I'll call you when I'm back in New York City."

"Ok." Brandy hung up the phone and did what Monay told her to do. Monay called the number Brandy gave her. Someone picked up within two rings.

"Hello, who am I speaking with?"

"Mr. White, may I ask who I am talking with?"

"Monay… so I see Mr. White, that Manny has you on his payroll."

"I'm not on nobody's payroll, Monay."

"So, what is your business with Brandy?"

"Just a few questions about a case she may be able to help us out with."

"I'll see you very soon, Mr. White." Monay hung up the phone and when she turned around, Pillz was standing there looking at her.

"So, you are going back to New York?"

"I have to, Pillz, they are after Brandy right now, I can't let them hurt her, because of us."

"I have someone in New York that can help."

"Baby, I told you who these people are. They are not street thugs, they rules are above ours, they live in a different world then we do."

"And so do Carmen, she's an ex-Marine, and she play by her own rules." Monay looked at Pillz when he said that.

"How do you know her?"

"We went to school together, she always had my back, and I always had hers."

"So why am I just now finding out about her?"

"She was in the Marine Corps when we got together, she just came home within the last six months. She ain't have nowhere to go, so I got her a house and the car she has, and I put her on my payroll."

"Shouldn't you have told me about her, Pillz?"

"Baby, she is a friend, nothing more."

"I believe you, but you shoulda still told me."

"You are right I should have but let me call her to take care of this problem for us."

"Are you sure you can trust her to get it done?"

"Yeah, I know she can get it done."

"Ok, I trust you. Here is the number and his name." Monay passed Pillz the paper and walked past him to go check on Promise.

Chapter 35

Jake walked up to Manny and handed him a piece of paper.

"What is this?"

"The address to whoever was at Monay's house, and what I was told, there was a plane ticket to L.A., so I'm thinking that's where Monay is hiding out now."

"And who lives at this address?"

"A Brandy Lawson."

"And I'm sure if she had a plane ticket from L.A., this Brandy person knows where Monay's house is."

"I'm sure you are right"

"Have our investigator bring her to us and let's see what she knows."

"I'm already on it, I told him to bring her to us. He's already waiting at her house right now for her to come home."

"Good let me know when you got her."

"Sure thing, Boss." Jake walked off, leaving Manny watching the polo game.

***

Carmen pulled up on the next block over from Brandy's house, she'd already talked to her and told her what was up. Carmen hopped the back gate, gun in hand and made her way to the side of the house. She looked inside the kitchen window to see the house was pitch black on the inside. She made her way through the back door, moving very quietly in the house. Checking every room, the house was empty.

She stood in the corner of the house in the dark and waited for Brandy to pull up. She saw lights from a car pull up in the driveway, she looked out the window as Brandy stepped out of the car. Brandy took her time walking up to her front door and taking the keys out of her purse. She didn't see Mr. White up behind her smoking a cigarette.

"How long you been house sitting, Ms. Long?" Brandy turned around as the sound of his voice made her jump.

"What are you doing here, are you stalking me?"

"No, I was waiting for Brandy to get back from out of town."

"Well, she not back yet and I would like you to leave now." Mr. White threw his cigarette down in the grass.

"No, I think I will stay a while, if it's all the same with you."

Brandy turned around and hurriedly put the key in the door. She opened the door, and Mr. White rushed her from behind, knocking her down to the floor. He jumped on top of her as she kicked and yelled.

"Get off of me, let me go." Mr. White put his hand over her mouth to stop her from yelling.

"Shut the fuck up, you don't think I know who you are, Brandy? You are going to take a ride with me. Someone wants to have a word with you." Brandy bit his hand.

"You bitch!" Mr. White smacked her so hard she stopped putting up a fight. He stood up over top of her and that's when Carmen came from behind him and put the gun to his head. Mr. White closed his eyes and put his hands up.

"I'm a cop. I can show you my badge."

"I don't give a fuck about you being a cop, move and I'ma blow your fucking head off."

"You don't know who you are dealing with, or who I work for."

"I don't care who you work for, and you don't know who you are dealing with." Before he could say another word, Carmen smacked him in the back of the head with the gun, knocking him out cold. His body hit the floor and just laid there.

"Brandy, get up and get me some tape."

"What took you so long to come get him?"

"I had to make sure he was by himself before I could do anything. Now hurry up with the tape." Brandy ran and got the tape and helped tape his hands behind his back and feet up before he woke back up.

Carmen pulled out her phone and called Pillz, after a few rings he picked up.

"Yo."

"I got him, what you want me to do with him now?'

"Hold on, let me give Monay the phone." Pillz handed Monay the phone. "She got him."

"Hello."

"I have a Mr. White here, what do you want me to do to him?"

"Can he hear me?"

"No, but I will put the phone to his ear if you want."

"Yes, I would like you to do that." Carmen kicked Mr. White in the face, waking him up. He let out a cry, then looked down at his bound hands and feet. Carmen bent down and placed the phone to his ear. "He can hear you now," she said.

"Mr. White, you are not having a good night, it's not going the way you hoped. Let me tell you what's going to happen, you are going to leave Brandy alone or next time, you will have two bullets in the back of your fucking head. I don't care about killing a cop, so I'ma let you play with the cards you deal."

Carmen put the phone back to her ear.

"What you want me to do to him?"

"Take him somewhere and drop him off. And tell Brandy to get the money from the other spot and take a plane back out here."

"I'll let her know."

"And take two pictures of Mr. White for me and send them to me."

"I'll do that now." Carmen told Brandy what Monay said and made Mr. White get in the trunk of the car.

"Brandy, get whatever you need out the house, pay some movers to pack your shit up and put it in storage, and get on a plane. These people ain't nothing to play with, they will kill you and dump your body in the ocean, tied down with bricks and chains."

"I'm going to pack up now and try to catch a plane out to-night."

"Good, let me go take care of Mr. White." Carmen got her car and drove off, leaving Brandy there packing her bags.

***

Dapp sat down on the hood of his car, smoking a blunt talking to Remo in the cut on a dead-end road.

"Remo, there is no work on the block, Pillz is MIA, Tee six feet under. Shit is ugly as fuck right now, homie."

"Shit is fucked up right now, and the block is still blazing hot right now."

"Who the fuck is at Tee spot right now?"

"I don't know, why?"

"Because the day he got popped, remember I gave him a hundred and twenty bands."

"So, you thinking the money still at his spot?"

"There is only one way to find out."

"We going for a ride?"

"Fucking right, let's see what Tee have at his spot." Dapp and Remo got in the car and pulled off, headed to Tee's house.

When they pulled up to Tee's house, his car was still parked outside, but his lights were on in the house. Dapp and Remo looked at each other and got out the car. Holding their guns, they walked through the back door of the house, but didn't see anyone, Dapp walked to his bedroom and saw Diamond laying in the bed. He knocked on the door to get her attention. Diamond jumped up when she saw Dapp standing there.

"How did you get in here?"

"Through the back door, it was unlocked."

"Who is in here with you?"

"It's me and Remo, that's all, what are you doing here?"

"Tee had me move in when he found out I was pregnant with his child."

"Diamond, you are pregnant?"

"Yeah, I am, and now my child is going to grow up without a father." Diamond started to cry.

"Don't cry, baby girl. I'm here for you, ok?" Diamond nodded her head.

"Thank you, Dapp."

"No pressure, ma. You know how me and big bro rocked."

"Yeah, I do." Diamond got up and gave Dapp a hug.

"Look, you good here, if you have any problems with anybody let me know. Here, take my number, just in case you need me for anything."

"Ok, thank you." Remo walked in the room a few minutes later and looked at Dapp and Diamond.

"What's going on in here?"

"Nothing, come on, let's bounce." Dapp looked at Diamond one more time before he tapped Remo on the chest.

"What's going on with her?"

"She's carrying Tee child. Did you find it?'

"Yeah, it was in the kitchen, under the sink cabinet and from the looks of it, it don't even look like it's been touched.

"Because the day he picked it up, shit went boom with him"

"So, what's the move now?"

"We find a plug to keep the ball rolling."

***

Carmen pulled over on a dark road with a bunch of woods surrounding the road. It was pitch black outside, she stepped out of the car and popped the truck. She looked at Mr. White laying there.

"I should kill you, but I'm not." Carmen pulled Mr. White out of the trunk, she cut the tape off his hands, and looked at him.

"You're not going to kill me, you just going to leave me in the wilderness, I might as well be dead."

"You keep talking, I can make that happen for you."

"Death don't frighten me, little girl. The question you should ask yourself is, if the tables was turned would I keep you alive."

"You know what, fuck this." Carmen put her gun to Mr. White's head and pulled the trigger, blowing his brains out. His body hit the ground and Carmen looked at him and shot him two more times in the chest. She got into her car and drove off. leaving his body in the woods, dead on a dirt road.

***

Brandy was packing her bags. She looked around the house to make sure she didn't forget anything. She walked out her front door and tuned around and to lock it. When she stepped off the porch, she was punched in the face. She was knocked out cold, her body was picked up and carried to the van that pulled up in the front of her house.

"What you think she did with White?" Jake looked around and shook his head.

"She killed him already. Come on, let's get the fuck up out of here." Jake got in the van and pulled off.

Chapter 36

Monay sat on the couch with her leg folded under her other leg. She had her phone in her hand. She texted Brandy three more times, before she put it together that they had Brandy. Pillz walked into the room and looked at Monay, he could tell something was wrong.

"Baby girl, what's that look on your face?"

"They have Brandy, I know they do."

"Carmen told me and you that she was Good."

"Something just don't feel right. Call Carmen and ask her to go check on Brandy for me please."

"I'm calling now to tell her to do that for you."

"Thank you, bae. Pillz pulled his phone out and called Carmen, after two rings, she picked up.

"Hello."

"Carmen, I need you to go by Brandy house to check on her for me please. She not picking up her phone."

"Sure, I'll go over there now to check up on her."

"Thanks, Carmen."

"No problem. And as far old boy, there was no saving him, he had to go."

"I'll tell Monay." Pillz hung up the phone and looked at Monay. "She killed White, she said she had to, there was no other way. And that's She Going to check on Brandy now."

"Thank you, bae."

***

When Brandy opened her eyes, she was laying on a couch with her feet and hands tied up, her hands was tied in front of her. Manny looked at her, as he was smoking his cigar.

"I hate I had to get you down here the way I did, but I think you know the nature of why you are here tied up on my couch." Brandy looked around the room, the only person that was in the room with her was Manny.

"Are you going to kill me?" Manny blow out smoke from his cigar and stood up.

"That all depends on our conversation, if you live or die." Brandy closed her eyes because Monay told her if they ever got her, no matter what they told her, in the end they would kill her, there's no winning with them.

"What do you know about my three hundred kilos of cocaine that was stolen from me?"

"I don't know nothing about no drugs. All I did was get paid to watch they baby."

"Where is Monay at now?"

"I don't know." Manny nodded and picked up the phone.

"Jake, come to the room and bring the buckets of water with you and the black chair." Manny looked at Brandy right before the door opened up. Brandy saw when Jake walked in the room with the chair and buckets of water. He picked Brandy up as she was trying to fight him off of her. He punched her in the face, knocking the fight out of her. He tied her down to the black chair and looked at Manny.

***

Carmen pulled up to Brandy's house she got out of her car and looked around. She saw Brandy's car was still out front, she walked to the door and saw Brandy's purse on the steps and the house key still in the lock. she picked the purse up and looked around before going in the house. She looked around the house, she knew then they had her. She walked outside to her car and pulled her phone out and called Pillz. After two rings, he picked up.

"Yeah."

"They got her, I'm holding her purse and car keys in my hands right."

"Fuck, I thought you told her to leave."

"I did. She musta come back to the house," she lied, because she had really messed up on this one.

"Ok, let me talk to Monay. Thanks, Carmen."

"I'm sorry, Pillz. I'ma try and find her."

"Let me know what you come up with."

"I will." Pillz looked at Monay. Monay knew what Pillz was about to say. Before he could say anything, she put her hand up to stop him.

"I'm going back to New York, we tried it your way, now it's my way."

"Monay—"

"Pillz, I'm going to get her dead or alive. Think about what she did for our daughter, she might die for being loyal to us."

"I'm coming with you then."

"No, I need you here with Promise. Let me do this and I promise, I will come back home to you." Pillz kissed Monay on the forehead.

"If you need me, I'm coming out there. Be safe, baby."

"Pillz, I will be." Monay walked to Promise and kissed her on both cheeks as she hugged her, before she walked out the door.

***

"Brandy, I don't want to hurt you, but you are leaving me no choice."

"I don't know where she is. I'm not lying."

Manny looked at Jake and nodded at him. Jake walked up to Brandy and put a towel over her face. Brandy was trying to kick and break loose as Jake held the towel over her face.

"Just know you made me do this to you, Brandy. I'm really a nice guy, but you forced my hand." Manny picked the bucket of water up and poured it over Brandy's face. Brandy was kicking and shaking as he poured the water over her face. Manny placed the bucket down on the ground. "Take the towel off her face, Jake." Brandy was spitting up water, her eyes were bloodshot red, she was taking deep breaths. Manny and Jake just looked at her.

"Brandy that was just one bucket of water, next go-round it will be two. Now let's try this again, shall we? Where is Monay at? And I want you to think about this, we know you came from L.A., we have your plane ticket." Brandy had tears in her eyes because she knew they were going to kill her, so she made her peace with God before she said anything.

"Fuck both of y'all, y'all can go to hell." Manny nodded at Jake as he put the towel over her face again. Manny picked up another bucket of water and started pouring it over her face again. Brandy as shaking Manny continuously poured the water on her face. Soon after, her face was pale blue. Manny looked at her lifeless body then at Jake.

"Dump her body off on the side of the road somewhere so Monay can see it on the news."

"I'll do it now, Boss." Manny walked to his office and sat down and lit a cigar.

Chapter 37

"Dee, what's shaking, homie?" Dee was sitting on the steps smoking a blunt when Speedy walked up to him.

"I'm just putting all of this shit together. I still don't know why Munchie would crash out like that. What the fuck was he thinking?" Dee passed Speedy the blunt.

"Munchie went out like a true gangster... he went up to the hospital and caught his body. He ain't give a fuck about no police, he had one nigga in his eyes, and he popped the bottle when he seen him, hands down."

"Yeah, now you got the nigga Dapp riding around like he is the king of the Ville, on the set, niggas need to pop his ass." Speedy passed the blunt back.

"So, why the fuck we talking about it? Let's find this nigga and pop his ass."

"Yo, dead ass, let's go take care of the business." Dee stood up and pulled his gun out. "Fuck it, Speedy, let's go catch a body."

"That's what the fuck I'm talking about, bang-bang season, let's go put that nigga in a fucking grave, homie." Speedy pulled his Gun out to show Dee he was holding.

***

Monay walked into Brandy's house and looked around seeing her suitcase at the front door. She walked out the door back to her car and pulled off. She parked across the street from Manny's detail shop and called him, after a few rings he picked up the phone.

"I was going to see how long it was going to take for you to call me."

"Where is Brandy at, Manny?"

"Monay, you're not new to this, we both know where she is, and we both know how this is going to end with the both of us." Monay nodded to herself and hit her hand on the arm rest of the car.

"It's going to end with me standing over your dead body and Jake begging for me to kill him, for what I have planned for him." Monay hung up the phone and drove off. Manny smiled as he lit up his cigar, Jake walked into the office.

"She's back from wherever she was at." Jake placed a newspaper down on Manny's desk. Manny picked up the paper and the headline read: *Dead Cop found on Zion Street Shot to Death.* Manny looked at Jake.

"Yeah, that was our guy, the thing about it is Monay ain't kill him, someone else did."

"It don't matter who killed him, he's dead. That's three cops who worked for us within the last few years. We need her dead yesterday."

"How you want to take care of it?"

"Let me make a few calls and get back to you on that. But as of right now, get some more men down here just in case she tries something."

"Sure thing, Boss."

Chapter 38

Remo walked out of the deli eating a breakfast sandwich, headed down Albany Avenue to Smith Street, when Speedy came walking from the path and saw him.

"Yo Remo, pull up."

"Come on, nigga. Don't act like we fuck with each other. What the fuck you want?"

Speedy licked his lips and nodded as he walked up to Remo. Remo stood his ground, as he looked at Speedy in the eyes.

"You right, we don't fuck with each other, but check this out." Speedy pulled his gun out and placed it to Remo's stomach. Remo just looked at Speedy. "Tell your fucking owner Dapp, Munchie ain't going to die alone and when we see that nigga, it's get ready for the murder one game."

Yeah, nigga, I got you."

"One more thing."

"And what the fuck is that?" Speedy looked At Remo and smiled then smacked him in the face with the gun knocking him down to the ground. Speedy pointed the gun at Remo. "Next time we meet, just know there's no more talking, fuck boy."

Speedy put his gun back in his waist and walked back through the path, leaving Remo on the ground.

***

Monay pulled out her phone and called Carmen.

"Hello."

"Hey, it's Monay."

"Hey, what's up?"

"I was seeing if you can meet up with me at Avon Lake within the hour."

"Sure, I'm on my way there now."

"Cool, I'll be waiting for you to get here, beautiful." Monay hung up the phone and leaned up against her car as she waited for Carmen. She knew killing Manny wasn't going to be easy, she also knew he wasn't going to stop coming for them. Monay looked at her watch and saw it was 8:35 pm, that's when she saw Carmen's car coming down the road. Carmen pulled over next to her and she waited for Carmen to step out of the car. When Carmen walked up to her, Monay gave her a hug.

"Hey, I'm sorry about your friend, but I told her to leave. I don't know why she stayed."

"It's alright and thank you for all you are doing for us. But I need your help, Carmen."

"Sure, anything, what's up?"

"Manny's not going to stop coming at me or Pillz, the only way to stop him is to stop his heart from pumping. And I know by now, he'll have more men with him. The only way to get him is at his house and I don't know where that is, but I know that's the only place he will be at with his guard down."

"So what, you want me to follow him, then kill him?"

"No, I want to kill everyone that's with him, then kill him. I don't want nobody to be left alive."

"You are cold-hearted, but I like the way you think. Come on, we can take this car. It's stolen, but it won't be reported for another seventy-two hours. So that gives us enough time to kill them, then burn the car."

"Carmen, I don't know why I'm just meeting you, but I love your style." Monay got into the car with Carmen, Carmen played the remix of "Never Scared" with Jadakiss and looked at Monay and smiled before driving off.

***

"So, these niggas have that much heart to run up on you with the hammer, like shit is sweet with us?" Dapp looked at Remo, who held the wet face rag to his head where he was smacked in the head. "This nigga Speedy was by himself?"

"Fucking right, but he cut through the path, and I'm thinking if he cut through the path, the only place he was going was Dee's spot."

"Let's go pay that nigga a visit then, and we ain't doing no talking, we pulling up and blasting. If niggas want beef, we pulling up the strong way."

"Fuck it, let's ride out on these niggas."

"We out, come on." Dapp and Remo got in the car and pulled off.

***

"Wait, hold up, you telling me you had this fool down bad and you ain't clap him?"

"It was too many eyes, Doggy, so I just smacked him in the face with the burner to let him know shit is real. And I told him to let Dapp know it's murder season and Munchie ain't dying alone." Sitting on the steps, all he could do was laugh as he smoked his blunt.

"You know them niggas might have enough heart to come back blasting."

"Shit, let them come, I don't give a fuck about catching a body, them boys ain't got enough heart to pull up on this block with the dumb shit."

"Speedy, I don't put shit past nobody, but let them fuck up and die today."

"Man, fuck them. Roll up a blunt, I'm trying to get high, homie."

"Copy that." Dee broke the L down and started rolling up a blunt.

"Dapp, that's them niggas, thinking shit is sweet smoking a blunt on the step, like we wasn't going to pull back up."

"Man, fuck that, we ain't come to talk, let's let these niggas know shit is real." Remo pulled out his gun and looked at Dapp. Dapp shook his head and pulled his gun out.

"What's the word for tonight?"

"Shit, I'm trying to fuck something, homie, so you know I'm about to push off."

"Speedy, you stay with your dick in a bitch."

"I'm living the American Dream, fucking bitches, getting money and staying high. It don't get no better than this." Dee started laughing.

Dapp and Remo ducked down behind a car, Dapp nodded at Remo, that's when the both of them jumped from behind the car. Dee looked at them and hit Speedy on the chest. Dapp was shooting at Dee as Remo was shooting at Speedy. Speedy jumped off the steps, ran behind a tree and started to shoot back. Dee pulled his gun out and started shooting at Dapp. Dapp ducked down behind the car as he reloaded his gun. Dee jumped off the steps and ran behind the house. Remo ran back to where Dapp was.

"Come on, man, we got to get the fuck from out of here now before them boys in blue come."

"Man, fuck that. I ain't leaving till one of them bitch ass nigga is dead."

"Dapp, you tripping. Come the fuck on, now."

"What the fuck I just say, Remo?" Remo went to get up from behind the car and when he turned around, Speedy was pointing his gun at his head. Remo didn't get to say a word as the bullets was ripping through. Dapp turned around and fired two shots, hitting Speedy in the arm and grazing his face.

Speedy took off running behind the house. Dapp got up and just looked down at Remo's dead body. He turned his head and saw the police coming his way. He started to shoot at them, shooting the car windshield out. The cop car hit a parked car, and Dapp took off running down the street.

Chapter 39

Jake walked to the back office where Manny was,he had a few men standing around him.

"There's no sign of Manny nowhere, Boss."

"Get the cars ready, and let's get out of here for tonight." Manny walked outside and looked around before getting in the back seat of the car. Jake closed the car door and walked around to the front of the car and got inside. Three cars pulled off from the back of the detail shop. Manny lit his cigar.

"So where do you think she is at now?"

"Watching us, I wouldn't put it past her."

"So, you think she following us?"

"No, she want to catch me in the open, where the ball is in her hands."

"That makes senses, so we just need to be on point around the detail shop."

"We have to, till we kill the bitch, Jake."

"I'll make sure we have extra men around the detail shop at all times."

"Good."

Monay and Carmen followed Manny's car for twenty-five minutes on the turnpike.

"You think they know we are following them?"

"No, Carmen, we are too many cars back, but I don't think they are going to Manny's house, I think they are going somewhere else."

"What car do you think he is in?"

"Without question, he's in the middle car."

"So, you want to try and catch them on the highway?" Carmen looked at Monay and smiled.

"It will be too risky, police, state trooper. It's best we catch them at the house, Carmen."

"Monay, they are cutting down that private road. If we go behind them, they will know we are following them."

"I know, pull over to the right, we have to walk the rest of the way."

Manny car came to a stop in front of his house Jake got out and opened his car door for him. All his guards stepped out the car guns in hand and walked up to Manny.

"What's your orders, Manny?"

"I'm good here for tonight, Jake. Just keep two guys out front and be back to pick me up tomorrow morning by 10:00 am."

"You two, y'all are here for the night, the rest of y'all be back here by 10:00 am tomorrow morning, you heard the boss." Manny walked to his front door and opened it up, he looked back at the men in his front yard and nodded before closing the door.

"Carmen, you see the two cars leaving?" Carmen looked at both cars and saw only four guards inside.

"Yeah, I see them driving off now."

"It was six of them altogether, it's four now, so that means he has two of them at the house with him." Monay and Carmen made their way through the woods to Manny's house. They stopped at the back gate when they saw both men walking around the house, holding AR-15's.

"So how you want to do it, Monay?"

"Let them walk around the house one more time. You see the window right there? That's our way in the house." Monay watched as the two guards turned the corner to the house. She nodded at Carmen, and both of them jumped the gate and ran to the side of the house. Carmen opened up the window for Monay to climb through it. Once Monay was inside, she helped Carmen through the window, they closed the window right before the guards came back around.

Monay looked around the house, she pointed upstairs where she heard noise. They walked up the stairs step by step. When they reached the top of the steps, Carmen pointed at the room where the lights were on. Monay looked through the crack of the door and saw Manny sitting on the bed fresh out the shower. She opened the door with her gun pointed right at his head. Carmen walked behind her with her gun pointed at him as well. Manny's eyes got as big as half-dollar coins when he saw them walk in the room.

"Did I catch you at a bad time, Manny?"

"I see I underestimated you, Monay. So what, you going to shoot me in the head or chest?" Manny looked at Carmen, who was standing there pointing her gun at him, not saying a word.

"That would be too easy for you, Manny, you really musta forgot who the fuck I really was. I do shit to motherfuckers the devil ain't think of yet" Manny went to jump up at Monay, when Carmen smacked him in the back of the head with the gun, knocking him to the floor. He fell in front of Monay, he looked up at her as she kicked him in the face, knocking him out cold.

"Help me tie him up, and I hope you got a stomach for what you are about to see." When Manny opened his eyes, he had tape over his mouth, and he was tied down to the bed. He looked up at Monay with a knife in her hands. Her shirt was off, all he saw was her black lace bra. He looked over at Carmen as she stood next to the door with her arms crossed watching Monay.

Manny, I'm letting you know this now. This is going to hurt very bad, but you kept coming after me, so this is what you wanted." Monay took the knife and ran it across Manny's stomach. She smiled down at him as she jammed it into his stomach. Manny's face turned bloodshot red as Monay had the knife in his stomach. Carmen couldn't believe what she was seeing, and how Monay was enjoying herself.

SAYNOMORE

Chapter 40

Jake pulled up at Manny's house at 10:00 am, looked around at the two guards parked out front, and walked up to them.

"How was it out here last night?"

"Quiet, we walked the grounds all night."

"Let me go let Manny know we are here and ready to roll out." Jake walked to the front door and opened it up, he looked back at the guards talking as he went in the house and closed the door.

"Manny, we are out front waiting for you, you hear me?" Jake waited to see if Manny was going to say something, before he walked up the stairs to his room. When he pushed the door open, he covered his mouth and ran outside and threw up. All the guards looked at him.

"Jake, what's wrong, where is Manny at?" Jake didn't say a word he just pointed in the house. The two guards that were outside all night ran in the house to Manny's bedroom. They both stopped when they saw Manny on the bed covered in blood, his stomach cut open with all his guts taken out. His head was cut off and placed in his stomach with his intestines coming out of his mouth, with a message written on the wall in blood that said, "Sometimes you have to fight the devil with a demon. I'm coming for you next, Jake." Both of the guards looked at each other as they walked back out the house.

***

"Monay, I saw some crazy shit overseas, all kinds of killing, but I have never seen what the fuck you did last night to anyone in my life." Monay looked at Carmen as they sat in the park eating breakfast.

"Carmen, there are two different kinds of fear, just like there are two different kinds of respect. The cartel only respect fear. I been a part of that life since I was eight years old. I learned how to cut someone open and still keep them alive till I'm ready for them to die."

"How did you become a part of that life?"

"I was sold as a little girl to Omar, and over time I became whatever he needed me to be, and till it was a part of my everyday life. After so many years of the abuse and being treated like street working hooker, I found my way out I set it up and killed him and his worker and I stole three hundred kilos of cocaine."

"So now they want they dope back?"

"No, they want me back, it's not going to stop to I kill Big Country."

"Who is Big Country?"

"He's nobody. Come on, we been in the park too long it's time for us to go."

"Just know I'm here for you no matter what, girl."

"I already know, sweetie." Monay gave Carmen a hug before leaving the park.

"Monay, just don't ask me to do no crazy shit like you did last night and we are good." Monay started laughing.

"I won't, child."

***

Big Country looked at the pictures that Jake sent him of Manny. He looked around at the men in his office. "I told him not to be the one whose head ends up in a box. Box Stomach, it really don't matter where the head ended up, either way he dead."

"So, what about Jake, Country?'

"Let Monay be his problem. Maybe she might put his head in his ass, I guess only time will tell." Big Country walked to the window and lit his cigar.

"I don't care if she kills Jake, what I do care about is this bullshit can come back on us down here. So, what I want you to do is fly to New York, and if Jake ain't dead by the time y'all get there, then y'all go ahead and kill him and burn the detail shop down." Ghost got up and walked out the door with both of his men behind them.

SAYNOMORE

Chapter 41

Dapp sat down with his head down. Because of the hate he had in his heart for Munchie and his homie, his action cost Remo his life. Remo told him to come on, but he didn't listen. And just to look at Remo's face as the bullets were ripping through him, and to watch him take his last breath, hurt him more than anything. That was his day one.

He walked into the house and pulled the bottle of Ciróc out and started taking shots back-to-back, for his homie Remo. In the distance he could hear the police siren getting closer and closer to his house. He sat at the kitchen table rolling up a blunt, looked at his gun on the table and got up when he heard the police car tires stopping in front of his house.

He walked and looked out the living room window, saw the police officers jumping out of the car with their guns in their hands, so he walked back to the table and picked up his gun and made sure it was fully loaded. He dropped to his knees and said The Lord's Prayer, he knew there was no way out of this, he took two more shots of Ciróc, before he heard the bullhorn.

"Alex Smith, we have your house surrounded. Come out with your hands up, or we are coming inside to get you dead or alive." Dapp knew there was only one way his story was going to end today, he said to himself, "Nike's and up towns stomp the ground, Boogie Down Browns." He opened his front door and started shooting, hitting one of the officers in the neck, dropping him. He closed his front door and jumped on the floor.

As the house was being shot up, he got up and ran to the back door. He stopped and felt his side, he looked and saw the blood all over his hand. Then he licked his lips and took a deep breath, he knew in his heart he was going to die. He bit down on his teeth, ran towards the back door and swung it open. "Ya looking for me, here the fuck I am."

Dapp started shooting at all the police in his backyard. He dropped his gun, as he was blown back to the door, hit in the chest with the rounds from the shotgun. He looked at all the officers who had their guns pointed at him. Everything was in slow motion as he saw the sparks coming from the gun and felt the impact from the bullets hitting his chest. Dapp dropped down to his knees as tears came out of his eyes. He closed his eyes as his body leaned forward and fell over the steps, before one of the officers walked up to him and looked down at his dead body.

***

The street was blocked off with yellow caution tape, police cars were everywhere, CSI was out there and two local news teams. Sha-p and Tory walked up to Pretty.

"Pretty, please don't tell me Dapp is dead."

"Sha-p, the homie is gone, they flatlined the homie." Sha-p turned around and looked at Tory and placed her face on her shoulder as she started crying. Tory looked at Pretty with tears in her eyes.

"Pretty, what happened out here?"

"Word is Dapp and Remo had a shootout with Dee and Speedy. Remo ended up getting killed. When the police pulled up, Dapp started busting at them, he killed one of the officers in the car, and took off running. The other jumped out the car and ran behind him. He saw him run in the house, Tory. Dapp went out blazing, he took three of the officers out with him. He ain't die alone he went out clapping, that's on Browns." Tory had tears coming down her face as they took Dapp's body out the backyard.

Chapter 42

Jake sat in the detail shop, looking at the pictures of Manny he sent to Big Country. It's been two days since Manny's been dead, and he hadn't seen or heard Monay, but he knew she was somewhere watching him. Then there was knock at the door to Manny's office.

"Come in." Jake watched as Ghost walked into the office. Jake got up and shook his hand.

"I ain't know you was coming up here. Country sent you?"

"Yeah, he told me to come up here to see what's going on with Manny being killed and Monay."

"We doing all we can do to find her now, Ghost."

"And how is that coming along?"

"It's not."

"Don't worry about it then."

"So, what…we just going to let her walk away like she ain't kill and gut Manny the fuck out?"

"Yeah, just like that." Jake heard some noise in the shop. He got up and walked out the door and saw both of his men lying dead in a pool of blood. He turned around and looked at Ghost, as Ghost pointed a black 9mm at him with a silencer on it. Ghost pulled the trigger twice, killing Jake, he stood over Jake and shot him two more times.

"I want gas everywhere, I want this place burned down to the ground, now." Ghost looked at Jake's Body one more time and shot his body again before walking off. Monay and Carmen sat in the parking lot across the street watching Ghost and his men when they walked into the detail shop.

"Monay, who are them guys?"

"I only know one of them, the dark-skinned one, his name is Ghost. And if he's up here, that means two things. One, I really pissed off Big Country and two, nobody that's in that detail shop is going to come out alive." Carmen looked at Monay when she said that. Monay didn't say another word. Within twenty minutes, they watched as the black SUVs pulled out of the detail shop, that's when Monay saw the flames coming out the top of the roof. All she did was look at Carmen. She started the car and drove off.

"It's done, Ghost had everyone in there killed."

"So, what now?"

"I'm going back to L.A., and I was thinking you should come with me."

"You for real?"

"I am. Come on, me and Pillz got you."

"Cool, let's go." Monay smiled and drove off.

Chapter 43

Two months later

Pillz walked outside to the pool where Monay and Carmen were with Promise. He walked up to Monay and bent down and gave Monay a kiss on the lips as she sat down on the edge of the pool.

"Monay, I have to take a trip back to New York." Monay looked at Pillz then she looked at Carmen and handed Promise to her while she went and talked to Pillz.

"Why do you have to go back to New York? Everything is dead out there."

"Monay, I'm just going to pay my respects to a friend that's all, I'll only be gone a few days at the most."

"No, I don't want you to go. We all have a new life out here, you don't need to go back, that's the past, let the past be the past."

"Monay, a lot of people died because of me, there's nothing, I can do about that, but I can go and show respect to they resting spot."

"I don't agree with it, but if you want to go back and risk losing all we have here, then who am I to stop you?"

"Monay, you are my wife, my child's mother, my best friend, I'm just asking you trust me, and let me go show my respect." Monay closed her eyes and walked up To Pillz.

"I do trust you. Just promise me that you are going to come back home to us."

"I promise I'll come back home to my family."

Pillz kissed Monay on the lips and then walked up to Carmen and took Promise from her, looked into his daughter's eyes and kissed her on the forehead.

"Daddy loves you and I will be back in a few days, Promise." Pillz nodded at Carmen as he handed her back Promise, he looked at Monay standing by the table before he walked off to head to the airport.

***

Pillz pulled up at the cemetery and walked up to Munchie's headstone and kneeled down, he placed a picture of them together from a block party two years ago.

"Rest in peace, I love you, homie." Pillz got up and walked to Tee's headstone, he read the words engraved on his headstone. *Loyalty, Respect, a Big Homie and a brother to All.*

Tee once told Pillz, "It all starts with a penny, and we become loyal to the block to turn the penny into a dollar, we live for the dollar and die behind the chase for it." Pillz reached into his pocket and pulled out one penny and a dollar, the penny was for the beginning of the chase and the dollar was for the end of the chase. Pillz walked to Dapp's grave, it hurt to know he was dead, he was the one reason why they yelled Browns. he laid the Browns flag down next to his headstone and placed a rock over it to hold it in place.

There were no words that needed to be said. He walked back to his car. He heard the stories about how Dapp got killed and Remo. But now, there was only one place he had to go before he went back to L.A., and that was to go see Dee and Speedy, and there was nothing to talk about. Their actions killed Dapp and Remo, so now his action was going to be to kill both of them. Pillz pulled up on 43rd Street and got out of the car. He looked around before walking up to their door. He knocked two times before the door opened.

"What the fuck? Nigga, word was that you was out the hood for good, somewhere living the good life."

"Come on, man, you know how the streets talk. So, what's up? You going to let me come in or you going to keep me standing at the door?" Dee started laughing.

"Naw... come in, family. I ain't doing shit but smoking a blunt and watching this funny ass nigga Kevin Hart." Pillz walked into Dee's spot and sat down on his living room couch.

"Yo, what the fuck happened with you, Dapp and Remo?"

"You know niggas had to put that work in for Munchie, with no questions asked."

"My question is, who gave you the green light?"

"No one, we did what we had to do for the set, Pillz."

"That's the thing, Dee, you are a foot soldier, you not even a baby OG in the hood yet, and you and Speedy killed Remo on OG. And because of your actions, Dapp got killed by the boys in blue, and Dapp was the lifeline of Browns, who you think can carry the torch he held for so long?"

"Pillz, how they did Munchie was just foul hands down and that was the homie." Pillz picked up the blunt that was in the ashtray and lit it.

"Look, I fucked with Munchie dumb hard. I was the one who put him on his feet to supply the block, how you think he was eating?"

"I be knowing already." Pillz passed the blunt back to Dee. "Look, don't even worry about that shit. We are going to figure it out, homie, but I got to roll out right now."

"When you coming back?"

"You ain't going to see me when I do."

"Why you say that?"

"Because of how I'ma leave now." Dee looked at Pillz confused when he said that. Pillz walked to the door and when he turned around, he had his gun pointed at Dee's face, Dee dropped the blunt in a state of shock, before he knew it there was bullets ripping through his chest, as he was trying to catch his breath. Pillz looked at Dee as he laid in a pool of blood with his eyes open, dead to the world. Pillz walked out the front door, back to his car and drove away. All he needed to do was find Speedy, then he was on his way back to L.A.

***

Big Country walked out his front door when he saw Ghost pulling up. He walked up to him and placed both of his hands on his face and kissed both cheeks.

"Tell me, Ghost, how did it go with Jake?" Ghost kissed Big Country's ring.

"Everything is done. I killed Jake and his men and we also burned down Manny's house, all that you asked me to do is done."

"That's why I put my trust in you, I will never question your loyalty to me."

"I will never give you a reason to question my loyalty, sir."

"Trust me, I know this." Big Country placed his hand on Ghost's back, leading him into the house.

"Come have lunch with me, Ghost, my cook is preparing it right now. Come, I want to know all details about your trip."

***

Speedy walked into Dee spot, and couldn't believe what he was seeing, his right-hand man flat-lined, laying in a pool of blood with his eyes open. He clenched his teeth and shook his head as tears came down his face.

"No Dee, no! Man, who the fuck did this to you?" Speedy looked at Dee one more time and walked out the house. He had his gun in his hand, not giving a fuck. He wanted blood for his man's death and on the set, he was going to get it.

Chapter 44

Diamond was packing up the last little bit of her and Tee's things. She was moving out of his spot, that's when Pillz walked through the door.

"What's up, little lady, you going somewhere?" Diamond walked up and gave Pillz a hug, he hugged her back.

"Yeah, I'm moving to the other side of town. I don't feel safe here no more. Tee is dead, too many people know where he stayed. Plus, I'm carrying his child and I don't want nothing to happen to me or the baby."

"How far are you along?"

"Three months now."

"Trust me, you are showing in all the right places" Diamond slapped Pillz on the shoulder, playing with him.

"You better stop it, Pillz."

"You know how I am already."

"Come on, come take a ride with me."

"And where are you taking me?"

"Come on, you are asking too many questions now, beautiful. Just meet me in the car."

Diamond cut her eyes at Pillz and smiled.

"Ok, give me a minute and I'll be right out."

"You don't take too long."

"I won't."

Pillz walked outside to the car and waited for Diamond to come out. He played SWV's "Weak In The Knees" as he waited for her. A few seconds later, Diamond came walking out the house looking fly as hell in her Gucci outfit.

"Damn, you just keep getting badder and badder, Diamond, like what the fuck."

"Whatever, Pillz. You ain't going to gas me up, so again, where are you taking me?"

"To my old spot, I want you to check it out." Diamond looked at Pillz, smiled and started singing along with SWV as Pillz drove.

***

Speedy walked up to J.D. as he was standing on Great Neck Road.

"Yo, what's good, playboy?"

"Shit, just out here getting this early money on the block, what's rocking with you?"

"Shit, just moving around, yo who was that at Tee's house just now?"

"Dead ass, I don't know but it looks like Pillz from a distance."

"You know what, I had a feeling his ass was back."

"After what happened with Dapp and Remo, you off all people shoulda known he was going to pull up."

"That nigga bleed just like us, he ain't bulletproof."

"I feel you on that shit, anybody could die."

"Yo, J.D., let me get to stepping. I got some shit I need to take care of."

"Say less, homie, be safe."

"Always, Scrap." Speedy dapped up J.D. before walking off down Great Neck Road.

***

Pillz pulled up in the driveway at his old house in Freeport.

"Come on, let me show you the inside." diamond got out the car and looked around, and followed Pillz inside.

"Pillz, this place is nice, who lives here now?"

"Nobody, this is where I use to come to get away from everybody. Every room is fully furnished, go take a look around and tell me what you think." Diamond went upstairs as Pillz sat down at the kitchen table, rolling up a blunt. Diamond came downstairs a few minutes later and walked in the kitchen where Pillz was at.

"Pillz, this house is dope as fuck."

"Yo, thanks ma, this was my kingdom for a minute."

"So why you bring me here?"

"Real talk, I wasn't going to bring you here, but when you told me you was having Tee's baby, then I saw you packing up everything by yourself, I just put it in my heart to hold you down." Diamond had tears in her eyes. "Nobody never did nothing like this for me, ever."

"You good now, I'ma hold you down, you don't never have to worry about nothing never again. I promise you that." Diamond walked up to Pillz and gave him a long hug.

Pillz held Diamond and felt how soft her body was. He couldn't help but to kiss her forehead and hold her tighter. Diamond looked up at Pillz and kissed his neck, he put his hands on her shoulders and stopped her.

"Diamond, we can't do this."

"We are grown, Pillz, we can do whatever we want."

Pillz took a deep breath and looked down at Diamond.

"Pillz, just let it flow." Diamond licked Pillz' lips and dropped down to her knees. She pulled his pants and boxers down, held his manhood in her hand and started sucking on him. Pillz closed his eyes and let out light moans.

"Damn Diamond, what the fuck, girl." Diamond got up and pulled her pants off and pushed Pillz onto the couch and got on top of him, she placed his manhood inside of her.

"Oh, my God! Pillz, you are so thick, I feel you growing inside of me daddy." Pillz had his eyes closed and his hands on Diamond's ass as she was riding him. Pillz flipped Diamond over and placed her legs on his shoulders as he started to pump in and out of her faster and faster, Diamond had her nails digging into Pillz' back.

"Diamond, your fucking pussy is water…damn, I'm about to bust."

"Go ahead, daddy, bust in this pussy. Let me feel your nut inside of me." Pillz started grinding hard inside of Diamond pussy as he was cumming. Afterwards, he looked at Diamond and kissed her lips.

Diamond, I can't believe we just done that."

"Pillz, this is our little secret. Nobody has to know, baby." Diamond looked in Pillz' eyes and kissed him on the lips one more time.

"Diamond, get dressed." Pillz walked to the bathroom and placed his hands on the sink and looked in the mirror. He couldn't believe what he just done. He loved Monay with all his heart. He walked out the bathroom back to where Diamond was, looked at her and handed her seventy-five hundred in cash and the keys to the house.

"Look, this is your new home. The house is paid off, don't nobody no about the house, nobody. You are safe here. Do you want me to drop you off back at Tee spot or are you good here?"

"All my things at Tee house are packed up."

"So, call some movers and have them put it in storage until you are ready to go get it."

"Ok, I'ma stay here, Pillz."

"Cool."

"Am I going to see you again?"

"It's going to be a while before you see me again, Diamond." Diamond walked up to Pillz and pulled him close to her.

"Then there's no rush for you to leave, let's make this time we have a memory we won't ever forget." Pillz closed his eyes and fell victim to Diamond all over again.

Chapter 45

Speedy sat in his car on Smith Street, drinking   forty-ounce of beer, smoking a blunt, when two police cars rode past him, making a left on to Albany Avenue. He got out the car and threw the empty beer bottle in the field behind the church. He'd called from the pay phone at the Pinks store to let them know there was a dead body in the house on 42nd Street. Dee was his brother and he wasn't going to let his body just lay there and decay. He stopped on the corner of Smith Street and lit up a Newport, looking for Pillz' car to ride past.

***

"What's up, beautiful, what you got going on? How is baby girl doing?"

"Oh My God, you need to hurry up and come home, because I'm really ready to evict her ass, she gets into everything."

"You really talking about evicting my daughter, how do you sound, Monay?"

"Like a bitch who would pack her bags and put her on a plane to a desolate destination called I don't give a fuck."

"Yo, you are too much for TV, Monay, hands down."

"I am so for real right now, Pillz, please come get this child."

"Baby, I'm leaving tonight to come home to you and Promise. How is Carmen liking it out there?"

"She is loving it. When I tell you she is loving it, I mean she is loving it. She puts on her little two-piece and goes to the beach and shows off that hourglass body. And when I tell you she is a guppy in the water, there is no getting her out."

"It sounds like that's your bestie now"

"It just feels so good to have someone who moves like me. I love her so much."

"That's good. I'm glad you got a real homie but look, I'm about to pull up at EZ Deli and get something to eat before my flight leaves in four hours."

"That's good to hear, I can't wait till you come home."

"I can't wait to see you." Speedy was across the street when Pillz pulled up at the deli, he looked around at the block to see who was around. He pulled his gun out and watched as Pillz was getting out of the car, talking on the phone. He pulled the phone from his ear when he heard someone call his name.

"Yo Pillz, what the fuck is rocking, pussy?" When Pillz turned around, Speedy had his gun pointed at him, shooting. Pillz dropped his phone and took off running behind EZ Deli. Speedy was running behind him shooting, Pillz pulled his gun out and waited for Speedy to cut the corner. As soon Speedy hit the corner, Pillz shot him three times, dropping him, and took off running back to his car. He picked up his cell phone and jumped in his car and peeled off.

People were running around outside to see what was going on. Monay was still on the phone yelling Pillz name. Two people ran to the back of the deli where Speedy took off running behind Pillz, when they got back there, he was gone.

Chapter 46

Diamond heard a knock at the door. She got off the couch and went to answer it, when she opened the door, she was looking at Carmen.

"Hello, can I help you?"

"Yes, my car broke down in front of your house, and my cell phone is dead, can I use your phone please?"

"Sure, come inside, let me go get it for you." Diamond walked to the room to get her cell phone as Carmen closed the front door. When Diamond came back to the living room, she stopped in her tracks as Carmen had the gun pointed at her.

"Pillz did a nice thing putting you up in this nice house he does have a good heart, but where you fucked up at was putting your pussy on his dick. Now, walk upstairs."

"Please don't kill me, I'm having a baby. Please don't, please."

Carmen didn't say a word, once upstairs, she pushed Diamond into the bathroom. "Get into the tub now."

"Please, don't do this, please don't."

Carmen watched as Diamond got into the tub, Diamond had tears coming down her face.

"Make your peace with God now."

"Please, don't do this, please don't." Carmen looked at Diamond and pulled the trigger three times, shooting her in the stomach, chest and head, killing her. She walked outside to her car, got two gallons of acid and poured it all over her body. She then went downstairs to the basement and lit two long stick candles, then she walked upstairs and did the same thing again. She looked at Diamond's body as it started to decay. She walked downstairs to the kitchen and turned on the stove's eyes, letting the gas fill the house up before she walked out the front door, locking it behind her.

***

Pillz jumped out of the car at the train station in Amityville Village. He couldn't believe Speedy almost killed him. He got on the train headed to the city. He wiped his gun down and threw it in the trash can, then he looked at his phone and saw he had twenty missed calls from Monay. He called her back, after the first ring she picked up.

"Pillz, what the fuck is going on out there?"

"Nothing, I'm good."

"Don't say that shit. I heard someone call your name, then I heard gunshots, don't lie to me, Pillz."

"Monay, chill out. I'm on my way to you now."

"Where the fuck are you right now?"

"I'm on the train, headed to New York City now to go to JFK, I'll be home in a few hours."

"Pillz, you are not hanging this phone up to your black ass is on the damn plane."

"I'm cool with that, bae."

***

Speedy sat in the path up against a tree. Pillz shot him in the shoulder and arm, he was out of breath. He was mad he missed his shot, he got up and made his way to the Flat Tops, before passing out in the backyard.

Chapter 47

Pillz walked into the house, Monay walked up to him and gave him a hug, and kiss on the lips.

"You are never going back to New York. Do you hear me?"

"Yeah, I hear you, baby girl. Now tell me, where is Promise At?"

"She is asleep in bed. Now how about you go take a hot shower, and I'ma go make you something to eat and it should be ready when you get out the shower."

"That sound like a plan to me. Hey, where is Carmen at?"

"She went out with some guy she met. She should be home later or sometime tomorrow after."

"It's good to know she's enjoying herself out here. I'ma go get in the shower now."

"Ok, I'ma make your food, bae." Monay watched as Pillz walked upstairs to the shower. When he was out of her sight, she picked up the phone and called Carmen.

After a few rings, she picked up.

"Hey girl, where you at?"

"On my way back to L.A. now. My plane leaves in two hours."

"Good, because he just got back home, Girl. He's taking a shower now."

"Did he ask where I was?"

"He sure did. I told him you was with a friend. What was he doing out there?"

"He went to the cemetery, then he took care of some dirty business, then I had to take care of some dirty business. I lost him while I was doing what I do, but everything is good now."

"What you had to take care of?"

"Not over the phone, I'll let you know as soon as i get there."

"Ok, I'll see you soon, beautiful." Monay hung up the phone and walked upstairs. She walked in the room and picked up Pillz' phone and went to his text messages and read one from Diamond.

Thank you for everything, Pillz, it really meant a lot to me, everything you done for me, and I do mean everything.

Monay placed the phone down and walked out the bedroom. Pillz got out the shower and walked in the bedroom and saw his phone was open to the text messages. He picked his phone up and when he turned around, Monay was looking at him with her gun in her hand, pointing it at him. "Pillz, I swear to God, I hope I don't have to tell our daughter her father died in a car accident. Tell me what the fuck that text mean, now!"

"Baby, you are tripping, hold up and place the gun down."

"Pillz, I swear to God, if you don't tell me what that text mean now, I'ma kill your ass."

"Monay, I moved Tee baby mother into my old spot so she will have a place to live, that's all."

"I hope so." Monay looked at Pillz and walked away. Pillz sat on the bed and placed his hands on his head. Monay walked back in the room and looked at him. With tears in her eyes, she looked at Pillz' back then called his name.

"Pillz." Pillz looked up at Monay. "You're lying."

"Monay—" before he could say another word, all he saw was the sparks and heard the bang as the gun went off.

The End

Lock Down Publications and Ca$h Presents assisted publishing packages.

BASIC PACKAGE $499

Editing

Cover Design

Formatting

UPGRADED PACKAGE $800

Typing

Editing

Cover Design

Formatting

ADVANCE PACKAGE $1,200

Typing

Editing

Cover Design

Formatting

Copyright registration

SAYNOMORE

Proofreading

Upload book to Amazon

LDP SUPREME PACKAGE $1,500

Typing

Editing

Cover Design

Formatting

Copyright registration

Proofreading

Set up Amazon account

Upload book to Amazon

Advertise on LDP Amazon and Facebook page

***Other services available upon request. Additional charges
may apply

Lock Down Publications

P.O. Box 944

Stockbridge, GA 30281-9998

Phone # 470 303-9761

Submission Guideline

Submit the first three chapters of your completed manuscript to ldpsubmissions@gmail.com, subject line: Your book's title. The manuscript must be in a .doc file and sent as an attachment. Document should be in Times New Roman, double spaced and in size 12 font. Also, provide your synopsis and full contact information. If sending multiple submissions, they must each be in a separate email.

Have a story but no way to send it electronically? You can still submit to LDP/Ca$h Presents. Send in the first three chapters, written or typed, of your completed manuscript to:

LDP: Submissions Dept
Po Box 944
Stockbridge, Ga 30281

DO NOT send original manuscript. Must be a duplicate.

Provide your synopsis and a cover letter containing your full contact information.

Thanks for considering LDP and Ca$h Presents.

<u>NEW RELEASES</u>

BLOOD OF A GOON by ROMELL TUKES
THE COCAINE PRINCESS 8 by KING RIO
THE MURDER QUEENS 3 by MICHAEL GALLON
GORILLAZ IN THE TRENCHES 3 by SAYNOMORE

Coming Soon from Lock Down Publications/Ca$h Presents
BLOOD OF A BOSS **VI**
SHADOWS OF THE GAME II
TRAP BASTARD II
By **Askari**
LOYAL TO THE GAME **IV**
By **T.J. & Jelissa**
TRUE SAVAGE **VIII**
MIDNIGHT CARTEL IV
DOPE BOY MAGIC IV
CITY OF KINGZ III
NIGHTMARE ON SILENT AVE II
THE PLUG OF LIL MEXICO II
CLASSIC CITY II
By **Chris Green**
BLAST FOR ME **III**
A SAVAGE DOPEBOY III
CUTTHROAT MAFIA III
DUFFLE BAG CARTEL VII
HEARTLESS GOON VI
By **Ghost**
A HUSTLER'S DECEIT III
KILL ZONE II
BAE BELONGS TO ME III
TIL DEATH II
By **Aryanna**
KING OF THE TRAP III
By **T.J. Edwards**
GORILLAZ IN THE BAY V
3X KRAZY III

SAYNOMORE

STRAIGHT BEAST MODE III
De'Kari
KINGPIN KILLAZ IV
STREET KINGS III
PAID IN BLOOD III
CARTEL KILLAZ IV
DOPE GODS III
Hood Rich
SINS OF A HUSTLA II
ASAD
YAYO V
Bred In The Game 2
S. Allen
THE STREETS WILL TALK II
By Yolanda Moore
SON OF A DOPE FIEND III
HEAVEN GOT A GHETTO III
SKI MASK MONEY III
By Renta
LOYALTY AIN'T PROMISED III
By Keith Williams
I'M NOTHING WITHOUT HIS LOVE II
SINS OF A THUG II
TO THE THUG I LOVED BEFORE II
IN A HUSTLER I TRUST II
By Monet Dragun
QUIET MONEY IV
EXTENDED CLIP III
THUG LIFE IV
By **Trai'Quan**

THE STREETS MADE ME IV

By **Larry D. Wright**

IF YOU CROSS ME ONCE III

ANGEL V

By **Anthony Fields**

THE STREETS WILL NEVER CLOSE IV

By **K'ajji**

HARD AND RUTHLESS III

KILLA KOUNTY IV

By **Khufu**

MONEY GAME III

By Smoove Dolla

JACK BOYS VS DOPE BOYS IV

A GANGSTA'S QUR'AN V

COKE GIRLZ II

COKE BOYS II

LIFE OF A SAVAGE V

CHI'RAQ GANGSTAS V

SOSA GANG III

BRONX SAVAGES II

BODYMORE KINGPINS II

BLOOD OF Λ GOON II

By Romell Tukes

MURDA WAS THE CASE III

Elijah R. Freeman

AN UNFORESEEN LOVE IV

BABY, I'M WINTERTIME COLD III

By **Meesha**

QUEEN OF THE ZOO III

By **Black Migo**

CONFESSIONS OF A JACKBOY III

By **Nicholas Lock**

KING KILLA II

By **Vincent "Vitto" Holloway**

BETRAYAL OF A THUG III

By **Fre$h**

THE BIRTH OF A GANGSTER III

By **Delmont Player**

TREAL LOVE II

By **Le'Monica Jackson**

FOR THE LOVE OF BLOOD III

By **Jamel Mitchell**

RAN OFF ON DA PLUG II

By **Paper Boi Rari**

HOOD CONSIGLIERE III

By **Keese**

PRETTY GIRLS DO NASTY THINGS II

By **Nicole Goosby**

LOVE IN THE TRENCHES II

By **Corey Robinson**

IT'S JUST ME AND YOU II

By **Ah'Million**

FOREVER GANGSTA III

By **Adrian Dulan**

THE COCAINE PRINCESS IX

By **King Rio**

CRIME BOSS II

Playa Ray

LOYALTY IS EVERYTHING III

Molotti
HERE TODAY GONE TOMORROW II
By Fly Rock
REAL G'S MOVE IN SILENCE II
By Von Diesel
GRIMEY WAYS IV
By Ray Vinci

<u>Available Now</u>

RESTRAINING ORDER **I & II**
By **CA$H & Coffee**
LOVE KNOWS NO BOUNDARIES **I II & III**
By **Coffee**
RAISED AS A GOON I, II, III & IV
BRED BY THE SLUMS I, II, III
BLAST FOR ME I & II
ROTTEN TO THE CORE I II III
A BRONX TALE I, II, III
DUFFLE BAG CARTEL I II III IV V VI
HEARTLESS GOON I II III IV V
A SAVAGE DOPEBOY I II
DRUG LORDS I II III
CUTTHROAT MAFIA I II
KING OF THE TRENCHES
By **Ghost**

SAYNOMORE

LAY IT DOWN **I & II**

LAST OF A DYING BREED I II

BLOOD STAINS OF A SHOTTA I & II III

By **Jamaica**

LOYAL TO THE GAME I II III

LIFE OF SIN I, II III

By **TJ & Jelissa**

BLOODY COMMAS I & II

SKI MASK CARTEL I II & III

KING OF NEW YORK I II,III IV V

RISE TO POWER I II III

COKE KINGS I II III IV V

BORN HEARTLESS I II III IV

KING OF THE TRAP I II

By **T.J. Edwards**

IF LOVING HIM IS WRONG...I & II

LOVE ME EVEN WHEN IT HURTS I II III

By **Jelissa**

WHEN THE STREETS CLAP BACK I & II III

THE HEART OF A SAVAGE I II III IV

MONEY MAFIA I II

LOYAL TO THE SOIL I II III

By **Jibril Williams**

A DISTINGUISHED THUG STOLE MY HEART I II & III

LOVE SHOULDN'T HURT I II III IV

RENEGADE BOYS I II III IV

PAID IN KARMA I II III

SAVAGE STORMS I II III

AN UNFORESEEN LOVE I II III

BABY, I'M WINTERTIME COLD I II

By **Meesha**

A GANGSTER'S CODE I &, II III

A GANGSTER'S SYN I II III

THE SAVAGE LIFE I II III

CHAINED TO THE STREETS I II III

BLOOD ON THE MONEY I II III

A GANGSTA'S PAIN I II III

By J-Blunt

PUSH IT TO THE LIMIT

By **Bre' Hayes**

BLOOD OF A BOSS **I, II, III, IV, V**

SHADOWS OF THE GAME

TRAP BASTARD

By **Askari**

THE STREETS BLEED MURDER **I, II & III**

THE HEART OF A GANGSTA I II& III

By **Jerry Jackson**

CUM FOR ME I II III IV V VI VII VIII

An **LDP Erotica Collaboration**

BRIDE OF A HUSTLA **I II & II**

THE FETTI GIRLS **I, II& III**

CORRUPTED BY A GANGSTA I, II III, IV

BLINDED BY HIS LOVE

THE PRICE YOU PAY FOR LOVE I, II ,III

DOPE GIRL MAGIC I II III

By **Destiny Skai**

WHEN A GOOD GIRL GOES BAD

By **Adrienne**

THE COST OF LOYALTY I II III

By Kweli

SAYNOMORE

A GANGSTER'S REVENGE **I II III & IV**

THE BOSS MAN'S DAUGHTERS I II III IV V

A SAVAGE LOVE **I & II**

BAE BELONGS TO ME I II

A HUSTLER'S DECEIT I, II, III

WHAT BAD BITCHES DO I, II, III

SOUL OF A MONSTER I II III

KILL ZONE

A DOPE BOY'S QUEEN I II III

TIL DEATH

By **Aryanna**

A KINGPIN'S AMBITON

A KINGPIN'S AMBITION **II**

I MURDER FOR THE DOUGH

By **Ambitious**

TRUE SAVAGE I II III IV V VI VII

DOPE BOY MAGIC I, II, III

MIDNIGHT CARTEL I II III

CITY OF KINGZ I II

NIGHTMARE ON SILENT AVE

THE PLUG OF LIL MEXICO II

CLASSIC CITY

By **Chris Green**

A DOPEBOY'S PRAYER

By **Eddie "Wolf" Lee**

THE KING CARTEL **I, II & III**

By **Frank Gresham**

THESE NIGGAS AIN'T LOYAL **I, II & III**

By **Nikki Tee**

GANGSTA SHYT **I II &III**

By **CATO**

THE ULTIMATE BETRAYAL

By **Phoenix**

BOSS'N UP **I , II & III**

By **Royal Nicole**

I LOVE YOU TO DEATH

By **Destiny J**

I RIDE FOR MY HITTA

I STILL RIDE FOR MY HITTA

By **Misty Holt**

LOVE & CHASIN' PAPER

By **Qay Crockett**

TO DIE IN VAIN

SINS OF A HUSTLA

By **ASAD**

BROOKLYN HUSTLAZ

By **Boogsy Morina**

BROOKLYN ON LOCK I & II

By **Sonovia**

GANGSTA CITY

By **Teddy Duke**

A DRUG KING AND HIS DIAMOND I & II III

A DOPEMAN'S RICHES

HER MAN, MINE'S TOO I, II

CASH MONEY HO'S

THE WIFEY I USED TO BE I II

PRETTY GIRLS DO NASTY THINGS

By Nicole Goosby

TRAPHOUSE KING **I II & III**

KINGPIN KILLAZ I II III

SAYNOMORE

STREET KINGS I II

PAID IN BLOOD **I II**

CARTEL KILLAZ I II III

DOPE GODS I II

By **Hood Rich**

LIPSTICK KILLAH **I, II, III**

CRIME OF PASSION I II & III

FRIEND OR FOE I II III

By **Mimi**

STEADY MOBBN' **I, II, III**

THE STREETS STAINED MY SOUL I II III

By **Marcellus Allen**

WHO SHOT YA **I, II, III**

SON OF A DOPE FIEND I II

HEAVEN GOT A GHETTO I II

SKI MASK MONEY I II

Renta

GORILLAZ IN THE BAY **I II III IV**

TEARS OF A GANGSTA I II

3X KRAZY I II

STRAIGHT BEAST MODE I II

DE'KARI

TRIGGADALE I II III

MURDAROBER WAS THE CASE I II

Elijah R. Freeman

GOD BLESS THE TRAPPERS I, II, III

THESE SCANDALOUS STREETS I, II, III

FEAR MY GANGSTA I, II, III IV, V

THESE STREETS DON'T LOVE NOBODY I, II

BURY ME A G I, II, III, IV, V

A GANGSTA'S EMPIRE I, II, III, IV

THE DOPEMAN'S BODYGAURD I II

THE REALEST KILLAZ I II III

THE LAST OF THE OGS I II III

Tranay Adams

THE STREETS ARE CALLING

Duquie Wilson

MARRIED TO A BOSS I II III

By Destiny Skai & Chris Green

KINGZ OF THE GAME I II III IV V VI VII

CRIME BOSS

Playa Ray

SLAUGHTER GANG I II III

RUTHLESS HEART I II III

By Willie Slaughter

FUK SHYT

By Blakk Diamond

DON'T F#CK WITH MY HEART I II

By Linnea

ADDICTED TO THE DRAMA I II III

IN THE ARM OF HIS BOSS II

By Jamila

YAYO I II III IV

A SHOOTER'S AMBITION I II

BRED IN THE GAME

By S. Allen

TRAP GOD I II III

RICH $AVAGE I II III

MONEY IN THE GRAVE I II III

By Martell Troublesome Bolden

FOREVER GANGSTA I II

GLOCKS ON SATIN SHEETS I II

By Adrian Dulan

TOE TAGZ I II III IV

LEVELS TO THIS SHYT I II

IT'S JUST ME AND YOU

By Ah'Million

KINGPIN DREAMS I II III

RAN OFF ON DA PLUG

By Paper Boi Rari

CONFESSIONS OF A GANGSTA I II III IV

CONFESSIONS OF A JACKBOY I II

By Nicholas Lock

I'M NOTHING WITHOUT HIS LOVE

SINS OF A THUG

TO THE THUG I LOVED BEFORE

A GANGSTA SAVED XMAS

IN A HUSTLER I TRUST

By Monet Dragun

CAUGHT UP IN THE LIFE I II III

THE STREETS NEVER LET GO I II III

By Robert Baptiste

NEW TO THE GAME I II III

MONEY, MURDER & MEMORIES I II III

By **Malik D. Rice**

LIFE OF A SAVAGE I II III IV

A GANGSTA'S QUR'AN I II III IV

MURDA SEASON I II III

GANGLAND CARTEL I II III

CHI'RAQ GANGSTAS I II III IV

KILLERS ON ELM STREET I II III

JACK BOYZ N DA BRONX I II III

A DOPEBOY'S DREAM I II III

JACK BOYS VS DOPE BOYS I II III

COKE GIRLZ

COKE BOYS

SOSA GANG I II

BRONX SAVAGES

BODYMORE KINGPINS

BLOOD OF A GOON

By Romell Tukes

LOYALTY AIN'T PROMISED I II

By Keith Williams

QUIET MONEY I II III

THUG LIFE I II III

EXTENDED CLIP I II

A GANGSTA'S PARADISE

By **Trai'Quan**

THE STREETS MADE ME I II III

By **Larry D. Wright**

THE ULTIMATE SACRIFICE I, II, III, IV, V, VI

KHADIFI

IF YOU CROSS ME ONCE I II

ANGEL I II III IV

IN THE BLINK OF AN EYE

By **Anthony Fields**

THE LIFE OF A HOOD STAR

By Ca$h & Rashia Wilson

THE STREETS WILL NEVER CLOSE I II III

By K'ajji

SAYNOMORE

CREAM I II III
THE STREETS WILL TALK
By Yolanda Moore
NIGHTMARES OF A HUSTLA I II III
By King Dream
CONCRETE KILLA I II III
VICIOUS LOYALTY I II III
By Kingpen
HARD AND RUTHLESS I II
MOB TOWN 251
THE BILLIONAIRE BENTLEYS I II III
REAL G'S MOVE IN SILENCE
By Von Diesel
GHOST MOB
Stilloan Robinson
MOB TIES I II III IV V VI
SOUL OF A HUSTLER, HEART OF A KILLER I II
GORILLAZ IN THE TRENCHES I II III
By SayNoMore
BODYMORE MURDERLAND I II III
THE BIRTH OF A GANGSTER I II
By Delmont Player
FOR THE LOVE OF A BOSS
By C. D. Blue
MOBBED UP I II III IV
THE BRICK MAN I II III IV V
THE COCAINE PRINCESS I II III IV V VI VII VIII
By King Rio
KILLA KOUNTY I II III IV
By Khufu

MONEY GAME I II

By Smoove Dolla

A GANGSTA'S KARMA I II III

By FLAME

KING OF THE TRENCHES I II III

by **GHOST & TRANAY ADAMS**

QUEEN OF THE ZOO I II

By **Black Migo**

GRIMEY WAYS I II III

By Ray Vinci

XMAS WITH AN ATL SHOOTER

By Ca$h & Destiny Skai

KING KILLA

By Vincent "Vitto" Holloway

BETRAYAL OF A THUG I II

By Fre$h

THE MURDER QUEENS I II III

By Michael Gallon

TREAL LOVE

By Le'Monica Jackson

FOR THE LOVE OF BLOOD I II

By Jamel Mitchell

HOOD CONSIGLIERE I II

By Keese

PROTÉGÉ OF A LEGEND I II III

LOVE IN THE TRENCHES

By Corey Robinson

BORN IN THE GRAVE I II III

By Self Made Tay

MOAN IN MY MOUTH

SAYNOMORE

By XTASY
TORN BETWEEN A GANGSTER AND A GENTLEMAN
By J-BLUNT & Miss Kim
LOYALTY IS EVERYTHING I II
Molotti
HERE TODAY GONE TOMORROW
By Fly Rock
PILLOW PRINCESS
By S. Hawkins
NAÏVE TO THE STREETS
WOMEN LIE MEN LIE I II III
GIRLS FALL LIKE DOMINOS
STACK BEFORE YOU SPURLGE
By A. Roy Milligan

<u>BOOKS BY LDP'S CEO, CA$H</u>

TRUST IN NO MAN

TRUST IN NO MAN 2

TRUST IN NO MAN 3

BONDED BY BLOOD

SHORTY GOT A THUG

THUGS CRY

THUGS CRY 2

THUGS CRY 3

TRUST NO BITCH

TRUST NO BITCH 2

TRUST NO BITCH 3

TIL MY CASKET DROPS

RESTRAINING ORDER

RESTRAINING ORDER 2

IN LOVE WITH A CONVICT

LIFE OF A HOOD STAR

XMAS WITH AN ATL SHOOTER

SAYNOMORE